small town
secrets

BOOKS BY ALYS MURRAY

small town
secrets

ALYS MURRAY

bookouture

Published by Bookouture in 2021

An imprint of Storyfire Ltd.
Carmelite House
50 Victoria Embankment
London EC4Y 0DZ

www.bookouture.com

ISBN: 978-1-80019-055-9
eBook ISBN: 978-1-80019-054-2

For Mom,
who taught me how to stand up, when to walk away, and what is
worth staying for.

CUT BACK FROM COMMERCIAL

STAND BY AUDIO

CHUCK: And we are back here at the top of the hour with some good news for all you single ladies out there!

CLOSE ON AMBER

INSERT BRIDE HOUSE.JPG PHOTO INTO LEFT SCREEN SLOT

AMBER: That's right, Chuck. If you're a single lady and you're looking for love... and a little more snow than we have here in Georgia, you might want to look into the Fortune Springs Settlement Initiative, which just launched in Fortune Springs, Colorado. After a recent census determined that their female population was well below fifty percent, they decided to offer jobs, funding and housing to any women interested in moving to their town and bringing gender parity back to their community. Sounds pretty good, right?

CUT TO WIDE STUDIO SHOT

CHUCK: It certainly sounds like an adventure, Amber. I'm only sad it's not a town of women looking for a guy like me.

AMBER: Hey, do you think they're hiring a newscaster out in Fortune Springs, Chuck?

INSERT WEBSITE ADDRESS IN LOWER THIRD

CHUCK: Oh, Amber, you know I'd be lost without you. But any women out there who don't keep me awake every morning at four a.m. when we start this broadcast should visit the website listed on screen for more details. And hurry, ladies! Because applications close at the end of this week.

Chapter One

I wasn't sure when, exactly, the road had lulled me to sleep. All I knew was that one minute, I was staring out of the window of the Greyhound bus, and the next, the collision of tires with a pothole jolted me awake. Wiping the sleep from my eyes, I checked my watch, nervous that I'd missed my stop.

No, it was only 12:15. Unless the bus was running ahead of schedule—something I couldn't believe, considering how late we'd been at our earlier stops—we'd be pulling in to Fortune Springs in just a few minutes.

I couldn't wait to stand up. After almost three days on a bus across this great nation, I was sick and tired of amber waves of grain and purple-mountains majesty. I wanted a hot meal, air conditioning that worked properly, and a chair that didn't make my rear end ache. I wanted something to look at besides the road disappearing beside me. I wanted to feel something other than unanswered anticipation.

That was the worst part, for me. The waiting. Knowing where you're going is a whole lot different than actually getting there, a fact I learned more and more with each passing mile. I knew *where* I was headed, obviously. Some small town in the middle of nowhere

Colorado called Fortune Springs. Surrounded on all sides by equally twee-named places like Edwards and Beaver Creek, the online brochure attached to my Settlement Fund application promised that it was the height of beauty, of tranquility, of rustic decadence.

The pictures I'd seen online delivered on those counts, but that wasn't why the knots in the pit of my stomach tightened with every minute it took to get there. Because what I really needed, more than a comfortable chair and more than rustic decadence, was a fresh start.

That, though, wasn't going to be easy. As I'd discovered days ago when I'd first seen a repeat of a newscast about it, the Fortune Springs Settlement Initiative was a scholarship or bursary fund of sorts, where the town—which apparently had a female population deficit—planned to select a few young women every year to come to their town, live in one of their houses for free, and get paid to (hopefully) stick around and start businesses or families.

The deadline for applications was a full month ago. But I hadn't seen the news story or the website's promises—full room and board for a year, a job or a small business loan and a living stipend—until it was too late. The minute I'd seen it, though, I printed out the application and filled it out, then recklessly caught the first bus heading west. I could only hope that, since this was their pilot year, they might have some space for me.

After all, who besides someone like me was going to come out here to the middle of nowhere in search of a new life? Only the truly desperate. Maybe no one was as desperate as me. Maybe no one else had showed up.

I had to hold on to that hope. It was my only chance. A long shot, really, more than a chance, but I had to take it. Or rather, I had to try. I wasn't going back to Savannah, Georgia, and I wasn't going back to him.

Virginia Bessel, get yourself together.

A shiver shook my shoulders, a miracle considering the sweltering heat of the bus. Thankfully, the driver's voice over the crackling loudspeaker pulled me away from cold, dark thoughts.

"Ladies and gentlemen, our next stop will be Fortune Springs. Please collect all your belongings. Next stop—Fortune Springs."

Most of my fellow travelers had gotten off the bus at the bustling Denver station, which left the aisles clear for me to shoulder my backpack and make my way to the front. I didn't need to pull anything down from the overhead racks, nor would I need to collect any belongings from the lower storage compartments once the bus crawled to a stop.

Everything I owned, I now carried on my back.

If any of the remaining passengers noticed this—or my teenage runaway getup of a hooded sweatshirt, ripped jeans, and broken-sole tennis shoes—none of them mentioned it. No one even looked up.

As the bus pulled to the curb, I kept my head low and considered thanking the bus driver. He looked tired. Run-down. He looked almost as bad as I felt. Thanking him would be the right thing to do, the kind of thing I would have done back in Savannah. But it was also the kind of needlessly polite gesture that was out of place in a crowd like this, which might have left an impression. The last thing I wanted was to leave an impression, to be identifiable in any way.

All of this—the cross-country road trip, the new life in a small town, the fact that I'd tossed my cell phone in a garbage can in Tupelo—was about disappearing. Not about being seen. I bit my tongue and waited for the bus to come to a complete stop before descending the stairs, taking the first steps into my new life.

Whatever I'd been expecting that new life to look like, what greeted me when I reached solid ground was *not* it. For one thing, the Fortune Springs stop was not in the middle of town, like the station in Denver, and not even on a main street, like several of the other small towns we'd swung through on our great journey across the country. Nope. This bus stop found me on the side of the highway.

I gripped the one good handle of my backpack as I scanned the horizon. No one in sight. Nothing but the surrounding scenery, the sight of which slightly improved my mood despite myself. Snow-peaked mountains and endless sky. Rich, clay soil and shockingly green grass. And just there, in the distance, I could just see the beginnings of a small town down below. The walk would be at least a mile. Maybe more.

Over my shoulder, I glanced at the retreating bus. Nothing for it now. I just had to get walking. At least I'd packed light.

Setting off, one foot in front of the other, my mind returned into familiar, defensive patterns. I had always tried to be one of those "look on the bright side" kind of people because, in my experience, if you didn't at least try to see the good in everything, all of the bad would swallow you whole. And at the very least, if seeing the good didn't solve your problems, at least it would distract you for a few minutes.

With every step, I tried to come up with something new, a positive on which to focus my energy. Out here, the air was fresh and clear, as if the Rocky Mountains had scrubbed the very oxygen particles themselves clean. That was a good thing. And my shoes. Old Converse sneakers were good for long walks. And the walk itself. All downhill. That was pretty good news, wasn't it?

Sure, I was walking towards an uncertain future where I might be quickly turned away. There was no guarantee that the days-long journey and all the risks I'd taken to get here would be worth it. But for now, for the moment, I was alone with my thoughts beneath a cool, clear, blue sky, walking towards a precious small town that looked picturesque even from a distance.

I couldn't remember the last time I'd been this independent. The last time I'd had such a say in my own future. That, alone, was enough to keep my footsteps light and my nerves from eating me alive.

About an hour and a serious misjudgment about the length of the walk later, I still wasn't regretting my decision to come to this middle of nowhere, hole in the wall town. I was just questioning the wisdom of not doing my research regarding where the bus would drop me once I'd gotten here. By the time I properly broached the first streets of the little neighborhoods on the outskirts of town, my shoes closed too tight around my swollen feet, and the cool spring air collected in droplets at my crown.

I was seriously regretting my bus-side wish of an opportunity to stretch my legs. Next time, I'd need to be more careful what I wished for.

Still, not all the aches screaming out from various corners of my body could distract me from the quaint charm of Fortune Springs,

Colorado. As I approached from the east, the distant, endless sky was brought to an abrupt halt by the interruption of towering, tree-dense mountains. Their snowcaps drew my eyes heavenward, then I followed the defined ski runs back down towards the town nestled at their base.

Almost in a trance, I moved forward now without even considering the pain in my shoes or the shortness of my own breath.

I'd never seen this much sky. This much nature. Not in my whole life. With that one look, I knew I loved it—the jewel-blue of the sky, the rich greens and browns of the mountains and the trees, the way the town seemed to have grown out of the earth like some kind of naturally occurring thing.

No. I stopped myself. That was a dangerous prospect, deciding I liked it here. Especially considering I wasn't going to stay. My plan had an expiration date. Despite the Settlement Initiative's hope that people who got the bursary would stay in town after their required year, I wasn't going to even wait until the ink dried on the final check they gave me. I would stay here one year. Long enough to fulfill my promise, get my money, and get out.

I wasn't the home-and-family type. I didn't want anyone pinning me down, didn't want to feel that I had to belong to anyone or anything. I'd done that before. Let myself be owned by another person. And the results had driven me here. I wasn't keen on repeating the experience again. Not now. Not ever.

But if the views of the town from the outside had been enough to make me get all poetic about the transcendental effects of the natural world, then the town itself, as I got deeper and deeper into its labyrinthine web of streets, was almost enough to get me to wax Hallmark poetic about the virtues of small-town life. *Almost.* As I walked the streets, trying to follow the natural flow of the houses towards some kind of main street—every small town had a main street, didn't they?—several folks assessed me with skeptical eyes, but waved and said "good morning" all the same. I did my best to let my own reply (a wave and a small smile) walk the line between polite and inconspicuous. I didn't want to make any enemies on my first few minutes in town, but I didn't want to make much of an impression, either.

Besides the friendly, if surprised, townsfolk though, it was the architecture of the town, the atmosphere of the whole place that got under my skin and stayed there. On the outskirts of Fortune Springs, the houses lined the streets with modern, rustic elegance, but the closer I got to the heart of town, the older those buildings grew. Sure, it had two whole traffic lights and wired electricity and everything else you'd expect from a modern town, but the buildings were constructed in that classic, Western settlement style. Some dark, timber structures soaked up all the light of the street, while some of the brightly colored shops and hotspots reflected it, nearly blinding in the afternoon sunshine.

It was all so beautiful. So simple. So painfully quaint and so obvious that the entire town had been built by love and determination. It was part real-life fairy tale and part Hollywood Old West backlot. The muscle buried in the left side of my chest tweaked painfully as I tried to school her enthusiasm back into cool indifference.

This place was a means to an end. It couldn't be anything more. I couldn't let it be.

At the center of town, my eyes fell down to the printed-out pamphlet about the Settlement Initiative I still held in my hand. I glanced in every direction, searching for the white-painted building in the photographs—the supposed head of the operation. The streets around me bustled with afternoon activity as people wandered from shop to shop and held their animated conversations, but no matter where I turned, I couldn't see any house that looked even remotely like the one in the brochure.

Or anyone who might be willing to help me.

The last thing I wanted to do was barge up to someone mid-conversation and demand directions. But with no phone, no map, and very little time left on my aching feet before they completely collapsed, I decided it was a risk I'd have to take.

At the junction of two streets—one called State Street and one called Commerce—I stood for a long moment, scanning the passing crowds for someone to approach. I needed someone sensible. Someone easy to talk to and easy to get away from. Someone who probably wouldn't remember me once this conversation concluded.

That's when I saw an older woman—70s, silver-haired and thick-spectacled—loading up groceries into the front seat of her car, which was parked in one of the painted spots just down the street. Bingo. Striding forward, I pushed the hood from my head and did my best to sound polite and harmless.

"Um, excuse me—?"

But I had been too quiet, too timid. Without turning, the woman slid into the front seat of her car, and at that exact moment, a man turned away from her trunk, apparently thinking I'd been addressing *him*.

My breath caught, and not just from the usual panic-mode my body flew into whenever a man gave me his full and undivided attention. This wasn't just a man. This was a monster of a man. Tall and broad and strong in ways I didn't know existed outside the pages of magazines, he towered over even my relatively tall frame, casting a long shadow over the sidewalk that only got longer with every casual step he took towards me. Sandy blond hair swooped across his forehead, and I had the strange urge to reach up and push it away from his face so I could get a better look at his blue-green sea glass eyes.

Of course, I would never do that. Not just because of the fear that had been my body's natural response, but because of his body. I tried not to think too much about it, but it was impossible to entirely ignore, really. The too-tight Fortune Springs Fire Department T-shirt wrapped around his muscles to great effect, and I had to wonder if that really *was* the largest T-shirt they sold, or if he preferred to show off the muscles that made up his towering form.

Something inside of me shuddered at the sight of him. There didn't seem to be a hint of danger lurking in the strong muscles of his forearms or the slightly crooked set of his lips, but I didn't exactly trust my own judgment when it came to things like that. The last one hadn't seemed dangerous either.

"Yeah, can I help you?"

My throat tightened. This wasn't the kind of attention I needed right now. From someone so direct and dangerous-looking. "Oh, um—sorry. I was just wondering if you know where the Harbin House is?"

I turned the pamphlet in my hands so he could see the picture. Partly in case he needed a visual reference, and partly to re-establish the distance between us and keep him away from me. The expression he had been wearing, an easygoing look of indifference, hardened instantly, and when his blue eyes returned to mine, the glass in them had been replaced by steel.

"The Bride House?"

Was that a note of disappointment I heard in his voice? Not that it mattered anyway. He'd gotten the houses mixed up. I tried to correct him, gently as I could.

"I'm actually looking for something called the Harbin House—"

"I know what you said."

Maybe so, but that didn't answer my question.

"Are you, uh, new in town? I don't know if I've ever seen you around here before."

There were unspoken gaps in his question, like he was hoping for an answer he knew he wasn't going to get. I shrugged and returned the pamphlet to my pocket.

"I'm new. Just going to turn in my application."

A snort. I flinched at the sound. "Calla'll be glad to see you, then."

I didn't like the sound of that. I bit the inside of my cheek to keep myself from saying something I'd regret. My spine went rod-straight.

"What's that supposed to mean?"

"Let's just say that there aren't too many people who would willingly chain themselves to this town. Or the people in it. You want my advice?"

There was something casual and easy about the gentle rhythms of his body as they moved into my space up on the sidewalk. Like he owned the town, like he knew every inch of it better than I ever could. Like I was an interloper, and he was the king sizing up a new subject.

Involuntarily, muscles twitched in my throat and in my legs. Flight response. Not because anything in this man was, on the surface, particularly threatening, but because the last few years of my life had taught me to question my own judgments, my own instincts. I counted to three, drinking in even breaths with every count, and squared my shoulders.

"I don't know. Do I?"

"I'd say you should get out of here as fast as you can."

It didn't sound like a threat. It sounded like a resigned warning. One that I wasn't going to heed. I needed this. I needed Fortune Springs. No one was going to run me out of town, not even this handsome, intimidating man in the too-tight fireman's T-shirt.

"Are you trying to scare me off?" His silence was answer enough. I decided to lie. "Just so you know, I'm pretty hard to scare off."

For a moment, he appraised me. "I can see that about you. You're going to be trouble around here, aren't you?"

"No. I just plan to live here. That's all."

"Right. You living here *is* the trouble."

I hated that cryptic remark. And I hated that it sounded almost sexy from his lips. I couldn't remember the last time I'd thought that about a man. Time to get out of here. Gripping my backpack somehow tighter, I approached the question again.

"So, where can I find the Harbin House?"

He pointed west, towards the mountains. I just hadn't gone far enough. "Down that street. It's the one that looks like a big wedding cake. You can't miss it."

"Thanks. For the directions and for your... hospitality."

Before he could reply—or do anything in reply—I turned on my heel and followed his instructions at the fastest pace I could possibly manage without breaking out into a full-on run.

Chapter Two

I wasn't going to let some slightly arrogant firefighter in a too-tight T-shirt ruin my mood. Or let hope slip through my fingers. I wasn't going to let him sway me. Not just because I needed this chance, but because I wasn't going to let him win.

I was so tired of letting men win. For once, I was going to claim my own victory. Small as it might have been.

So, when I finally found the picture from the brochure, sitting in the middle of that very real-life street, I lifted my chin and put on my best smile. The place was exactly how Tight T-shirt Man had described it. Like a living wedding cake, all white finishes and flourishes. I hadn't ever seen a house this big in real life, not even back in Savannah. Sure, I'd seen mansions in movies, but the pictures online somehow hadn't done the place justice. Once the front gate was opened, it gave way to a manicured lawn. The flower beds out front waited patiently for planting, but the green grass covering the front lawn flourished under the afternoon sun. A wrap-around porch encircled the entire property, and from the front porch ceiling, I could just barely make out the hooks for a porch swing. They were barren for the moment.

The entire place was striking and beautiful, haunting and slightly decaying. Large enough to quarter a small army, but somehow forgotten here in the middle of Main Street. It wasn't going to win any *Homes and Gardens* awards; I knew that. Still, it had potential.

It was beyond sappy to identify with a house, but as I carefully swung open the wrought-iron gate and stepped down the slightly crumbling concrete path up towards the front steps of the porch, I couldn't help it.

The house had potential. And maybe, so did I. Maybe my entire life had potential. But I'd only know if I took this first step and started over, here, at what the locals were apparently calling the Bride House.

The stairs out front groaned under my weight, protesting from lack of use, I imagined. And when I finally made it to the door, with its stained-glass window creating a slightly dizzying pattern of light across my skin, I rang the doorbell. Once. Then after a few moments, two and three times more.

No sound. I raised my knuckles to knock.

That did the trick. A moment later, the door flung open, revealing a woman in her mid-sixties whose stray strands of silver hair peeked out from beneath the brim of a broad sunhat decorated with embroidered flowers. Despite the state of the garden out front, her loose-fitting linen clothes seemed to indicate preparations for an afternoon outside in the dirt, but as she addressed me, her slightly amused eyes and smile competed for attention with her hands, fiddling with two dangling earrings, which she struggled to slip into her ears as she conversed.

"Yes, hello?"

"Hi…" I recognized her instantly. Her face was all over the website for the Settlement Initiative, but it felt rude to assume anything. "Are you Calla Holtzman?"

Calla Holtzman was the program's chaperone, and, the website had said, was in charge of making sure the women who applied were well looked-after. Apparently, she lived in the Harbin House—sorry, the Bride House—full-time. Her twinkling eyes didn't let go of mine.

"Are you the taxman or the police?"

"No."

"Are you here to sell something?"

"No."

Her face broke out into a wide, lipless but toothy grin. She held out her hand for a surprisingly firm handshake, suddenly the perfect, gracious hostess.

"Then, yes. I'm Calla Lee Holtzman. What can I do for you?"

This was the part I'd been dreading. The moment of truth. During the entire three-day ordeal that was the Greyhound cross-country bus, I'd practiced this in my head a thousand times, in a thousand different ways. By the time I'd crossed into Colorado, I thought I'd tinkered it to perfection, and memorized it so I could recite my plea by heart.

Unfortunately, the spotlight didn't look good on me. I couldn't find my words with a map and a flashlight. The sudden ache of importance gripped me by the back of my neck, practically paralyzing me.

I ran out of money two states ago. I didn't have anywhere to go. And even if I hadn't dumped my phone in a garbage can in Tupelo, I didn't have a friend in the world to call. This was the end of the line for me, and if I failed in this moment, I wouldn't have a clue what to do next. All of my hopes rested right here, on this porch, and on the woman staring at me from across the threshold.

"Um, well, I know this is going to sound a bit... What I mean is that I... it's past the deadline. But I didn't see your ad for the Settlement Initiative online until after it had already passed, and I thought that maybe we could... That maybe I could..."

This wasn't going well. Staring down at my shoes, I shoved the envelope in my hands forward. "Here. This is my application."

"Oh. I see." Mrs. Holtzman took the crinkling, slightly warped papers. Her expression and tone gave nothing away. "Well. This all looks very official. Very serious."

"I'm serious about being here."

Too intense. I cringed at my own voice, wishing that I could take back the last thirty seconds and start this whole conversation over again. A slight pause twisted between us, and I couldn't bear to look up and search her expression for answers, not when her tone remained so unreadable.

"I'm sure you know we've had a lot of interest. Lots of young women wanting to move here. Phone's been ringing off the hook with the way people are trying to elbow their way in."

"Oh."

My hands shook. I shoved them into my pockets. The house didn't look particularly occupied and the firefighter had made some comment about no one wanting to move here, but maybe it was still before moving day. Maybe he'd been messing with me.

"But why don't you come into my office and we'll have a look at all of the finer points, shall we?"

Without any other choice—without wanting another choice, really—I nodded and followed the older woman across the threshold of the house.

This had to be a good sign. Mrs. Holtzman wouldn't have invited me in if she was going to kick me out quickly.

At least, that's what I hoped was the case.

Stepping out from the porch and into the grand manor house, I couldn't help the way my mouth fell slightly open. The place was just as beautiful on the inside as it was outside, in a decaying, faded glory kind of way. Yes, there were creaking floorboards and chipping paint up on the ceilings, but if I ignored all those things, if I looked past what was there and instead saw what *had* been there, the home was striking.

To my left, there was a grand dining room linked to a smaller parlor. Before me, there was a grand staircase leading up to the higher floors. Mrs. Holtzman led me right, through a sitting room, past a swinging door, and into the kitchen.

It was like stepping through time, into a Victorian mansion where white-gloved servants delivered cookies and calling cards on silver trays. But the heavy-hipped walk and easy drawl of my host brought everything back down to earth, making it comfortable and homey despite the grand atmosphere enveloping us.

The marble countertops of the white-finished kitchen practically overflowed with food, and the scents of cinnamon and vanilla—had someone made sweet buns this morning?—caressed my senses. Somewhere in the middle of the culinary chaos, there sat an open laptop, an oversized travel mug of coffee, and a notebook and pen set.

"Oh, your… office?"

"Yeah, I like to be close to the snacks. Care for a seat?"

The fridge drew more of my attention, but I took the seat instead, not wanting to seem rude or needy. The thought of food, though, made my stomach growl. I didn't remember what state we'd been crossing when I'd eaten the last bite of my last sandwich, but I knew it wasn't anywhere close to Colorado. Calla's thinning left eyebrow rose.

"Now, that's what I like to hear. You hungry? What can I get you?"

When she said it, the words came out *what can I getcha*, which reminded me of an old-timey diner waitress and relaxed the tensely knotted muscles in my shoulders. Another good sign, right? Hopefully, they wouldn't kick me out mid-meal, right?

"Um, anything you have is great. I'm not picky."

Really, I wasn't. Sure, I had my favorites like anyone else, but during my last relationship, I'd learned to take what I could get and not ask for too much. Calla took this non-answer as an invitation to unload the contents of the fridge as she continued to speak.

"Alright. So." Lemonade hit the counter first. "You've come all the way out here…" Then a plate of decadent chocolate cake, three layers of sponge piled high with icing. "Without calling…" Next, an untouched rotisserie chicken. "And without emailing…" Some kind of dip in a slow cooker sleeve that smelled like bacon-cooked heaven. "And without turning in your application on time or receiving any kind of notice from us…" Iced tea, a bucket of salad, a handful of apples, and one chunk of sharp cheddar cheese. "And you want me to do what, exactly?"

It took me a full moment of staring at the food on the counter before I could formulate a full reply. My protesting stomach proved too much of a distraction.

"Well, I was hoping that you could—"

"Don't just sit there and look at the food," Mrs. Holtzman said, with a sardonic smile at the corners of her lips. "Eat it if you're hungry. My daughter, granddaughter, and my daughter's no-good boyfriend didn't show up for dinner last night. It's all leftovers, have what you like."

I didn't need asking twice. Immediately, I reached for the chicken, two slices of bread from the box at the center of the counter, and set about making a sandwich. I also pulled aside a slice of chocolate cake for good measure.

If I was going to get kicked out after this conversation, I might as well do it on a full stomach.

Proceeding to practically shovel food into my mouth, it took me a few moments of silence to realize how incredibly rude I'd been. I shot a sheepish look over my fork and winced an apologetic smile at the woman across from me.

"Thank you."

"You're hungry, aren't you?"

My pride kept me from confessing the truth, that I hadn't had a real meal in a few days. "I've been on the bus for awhile. Just haven't been able to stock up, you know?"

"I see. And where did you come from?"

"Savannah."

"Nice place, Savannah. Why did you want to come here when you could stay there?"

Suspicion rang in Mrs. Holtzman's voice, loud and clear as a fire alarm. The hairs on the back of my neck stood on end. I let out a breathy chuckle, though, hoping it would be enough to distract the old woman from the terror probably lurking in my eyes.

"Would you believe me if I said I was looking for a change of scenery?"

"Would you want me to believe you and ask no further questions?"

"It would definitely make this conversation easier."

Mrs. Holtzman settled her hands around her coffee mug, took a long sip, and raised a considering eyebrow.

"Interesting."

"Good interesting or bad interesting?"

Everything rested on that question. Good interesting might earn me a place here. Bad interesting might find me sleeping in a park tonight. Or taking the first bus back to the one place I couldn't bear to go. Hopefully Mrs. Holtzman couldn't hear the thundering of my worried heart across the small space between us.

"I'm not sure yet, to be perfectly honest. How about this: I'm going to ask you a series of questions that only require yes or no answers. I want you to answer them honestly, and with as much or little information as you see fit to give me, alright?"

I nodded. The stakes were high, but the deal seemed fair. Maybe even too fair. Mrs. Holtzman glanced down at the papers laid out on her makeshift marble desk, glancing at my slanted handwriting, made slightly messy by the fact that I'd written most of it on a bus.

"Is everything in this application true and real? Name, birth certificate, social security number, favorite movies?"

"Yes."

That, at least, I could answer honestly. Yes, I was Virginia Bessel. Yes, I was twenty-seven years old. Yes, I watched *The Princess Bride* and the fifth *Fast and Furious* movie probably more than the average person had any right to. Grew up in Ranburne, Alabama. Liked diner food and the color gray and the smell of warm, fresh-washed sheets. Guilty pleasures? Spy thriller paperbacks, low-stakes cooking shows, and those pastries you put in the toaster and then slather in fake-tasting icing.

Reason for applying for the Settlement Initiative? I'd even been honest about that. Maybe not *entirely* honest, but honest enough. *I need to start over.*

"And is your middle name really Excelsior?"

I let out a breath that sounded almost like a self-deprecating laugh. Talking about my mother or my past were not exactly my favorite things. "Yes. My mom was a bit of an eccentric."

"Was that why you left your hometown for Savannah?"

"No, I left because I wanted to go to college."

Mrs. Holtzman raised an eyebrow, her gaze still focused on the paper in front of her. "But you don't have a degree?"

"No."

That was all I wanted to say on that particular subject. Since Mrs. Holtzman told me I didn't have to elaborate, on this point, I wouldn't. Yes, I'd wanted a degree. Desperately. No, I hadn't finished one. Nothing more. Nothing less. I didn't trust anyone—especially myself—with too much of the truth.

"Hm." I didn't know if that was a good *hm* or a bad *hm*, but I didn't pry. "Are you…? Are you running away from something?"

A pause, a long pause. Then I made a decision. To trust this strange, weathered woman.

"Yes."

"Some*one*, more specifically?"

My chest tightened. So did my throat.

"Yes."

"Do you think that someone is going to follow you here?"

That wasn't the yes or no question Mrs. Holtzman seemed to think it was. Even before boarding the bus that would eventually take me here to Fortune Springs, I had spent my fair share of time mulling over that very same query. I still didn't have a satisfying answer, but I understood why it was being asked. Someone chasing me might eventually *find* me, and if Mrs. Holtzman was half the woman she seemed to be, she wouldn't want to intentionally put anyone else in this town in danger. Eventually, I settled on the only answer I knew to give.

"I don't know."

There was more silence then. Silence like before a life sentence was passed down to an innocent person on trial for a crime they didn't commit. I knotted my napkin in my lap, twisting and waiting for the inevitable swing of the executioner's blade.

The swing didn't come. Instead, Mrs. Holtzman leaned across the cool marble of the kitchen island and pressed her hand onto mine.

I flinched. Sudden contact wasn't really my thing. But when Mrs. Holtzman didn't retreat, I eventually relaxed under her soft, gentle touch. Then, I braved a glance upward, where the older woman was smiling that thin-lipped, understanding smile of hers.

"Your secret's safe with me. As it happens, we have… a few open rooms for the road-weary traveler looking for a fresh start. All of them, in fact."

A wave of emotion flooded behind my eyes. I blinked it away, trying to keep my cool as best I could. But I couldn't fight the excitement in my own voice. "Really?"

"I may have been exaggerating when I said women were beating down our doors to enter this program. The Settlement Initiative wasn't quite as popular as I hoped it would be, this first year. And I happen to have a soft spot for women like us."

"Like us?"

Mrs. Holtzman tapped the side of her nose. *I'll keep your secret, if you keep mine.* "I'm the one asking the questions here, Miss Virginia."

"Right." My lips twitched upwards. "Of course."

"So, what do you say? Are you going to come live with us at the Bride House? Stop your running for a little while?"

She couldn't know, not entirely, anyway, the gravity of what she'd just offered me. I wanted to beam, to throw my arms around her and cry and smile and thank her, but overwhelmed by feeling, I only managed: "I think I'd like that."

"I think you're going to like settling down here in Fortune Springs."

"Yeah, me too."

I returned the older woman's smile, but even as hope swelled and the promise of the future danced in the hazy, rose-tinted corners of her vision, I knew in my heart I was lying. I couldn't allow myself to like it here. One year from now, I'd be out of this place forever.

Off to somewhere that's sunny 360 days a year. Somewhere you could always hear the ocean.

I was beyond grateful for Mrs. Holtzman's bending of the rules. I was even more grateful for the woman's warm smile and understanding secret keeping. But that gratitude couldn't last forever.

No, maybe not forever. But when I dropped down into the downy-soft bed—a bed that was all mine for now—the pent-up tension of the last few days finally broke. I'd jumped, and I'd found somewhere soft to land.

And for now, that was enough.

Chapter Three

On my first night in the Bride House, I went to bed early, as instructed by Mrs. Holtzman. The woman walked a fine line between doting grandmother and drill instructor, and when she mentioned "resting" and "regaining your strength before making your debut out in town," I didn't even question it.

The bedroom I had been allocated sat at the farthest end of the second-floor hallway, past plain white-plaster walls and seemingly endless doorways. Once we were inside my new room, Mrs. Holtzman apologized for it. A simple bed, a simple desk, a few windows with lacy curtains, and end tables and lamps on either side. An empty photo frame on the chest of drawers. Everything was built in shades of rich wood and would have gone for a killing in any antique store in Savannah, but that wasn't what I loved about it.

It was mine. That's why I loved it. Mrs. Holtzman could apologize all she wanted, but I wouldn't hear it. The place was perfect.

Once I was alone, I spent most of the night reading the Bride House handbook—*expect lots of fun mixers to integrate you into the town! Make sure to be home by midnight!*—and drinking in the sounds of the old place. The creaking of floorboards and the muffled rumble of a television. The soft clinking of ice in a sweet tea glass. The whistle of the kettle as the hour grew later and later. The orchestra of the house lulled me to sleep, and, if I was being honest, it was the best sleep I'd had in years.

Usually, when I even managed to sleep, I'd gotten used to the sensation of waking up in a cold sweat. Of waking up from nightmares. Of waking up with breath so short and a chest so tight I wondered if I'd been strangled in my sleep.

But on my first morning in the Bride House, I woke to the sensation of warm, golden, mountain-filtered sunshine on my cheeks… and the scent of fresh pancakes frying in butter. As if pulled by the combination of grease and maple, I didn't waste any time, throwing on my hoodie over my pajamas and wandering downstairs to the kitchen. My quick pace almost kept me from taking in the sights of the old Victorian home all around me—its faded rugs tossed over creaking floorboards and the old, framed black and white photographs documenting Fortune Springs' town history.

Considering it was only myself and Calla in the house, I guess I expected the house to have an eerie kind of quiet. The echoing of a space too big for two people to share on their own. But just like last night, when I'd fallen asleep to the sounds of Calla downstairs, this morning, I found the air as full of sound as it was of pancake smell. A radio playing tinny, Johnny Cash country music. The crack of eggs against a pan. The sizzle of bacon. The rush of an extractor fan. The sounds of the street through an open window.

You'd have thought the house was full of life. That it was a home instead of a holding place for two strangers. The sound relaxed me a bit. The last time I'd shared a house with one other person, I'd crept around carefully, knowing one errant sound—the radio or a floorboard, a hum or a crack—would get me in trouble. Here, the air tingled with the promise of noise. Creeping down the stairs, I made my way into the kitchen, towards the source of it all.

Once I arrived, I saw Calla, poring over four active pans on the stove, each containing their own breakfast item. Eggs. Bacon. Sausage. Pancakes. Somewhere over her shoulder, the toaster popped, too.

"Morning, Virginia! How'd you like your eggs?"

One egg white, no salt. That's how I used to order my eggs. But after my experiment with going to sleep on a full belly yesterday, I must have been drunk on carbohydrates and sugar, because I heard myself say:

"Could I get three scrambled eggs, please?"

"Sure thing. You want cheese with those?"

A voice in the back of my head, a familiar, male voice, told me absolutely not. Out of habit more than anything else, I checked over my shoulder. No. Foolish. Of course he wasn't here. I'd run away to escape him.

What good was running away if I didn't do anything with that freedom? Even if the rebellion was small like this one?

"Yes, please. Lots of cheese."

"That's how I like mine, too. Glad to see you're not still full from dinner last night. I usually only cook for a crowd, or myself, so there's not a whole lot of in-between with my cooking, as you can see."

As Calla set about the work of finishing up breakfast, I slid onto one of the counter barstools to watch her from afar. In the handbook she'd given me last night about the Settlement Initiative, I'd read that breakfast and dinner would be provided every day, but I'd expected something like protein bars, or maybe a fruit tray. It was a lot of work for someone to go through, cooking all of this food, unless they were used to it.

"Do you have a big family?" I asked, peering over her shoulder as her easy hands maneuvered the pans and the flames of the stovetop.

"Used to." Something about the combination of her smile and those sad words sent shockwaves of pain right through me. Strange. I couldn't remember the last time I'd felt for anyone like that. So much of my life lately had been taken up by just surviving that there wasn't much room for anything else. "And I cook for lots of the town functions. None of the men in this town know anything about cooking. What about you? Lots of family?"

"I wrote about it on my application."

She slipped the eggs easily onto two plates, then followed with the pancakes and the rest of the ingredients, until each one was a small mountain of breakfast. Then, she took her place at the seat across from me. "If I'd wanted to hear it from the application, I would have made the application breakfast. It probably wouldn't have sassed me so much."

For a moment, I busied myself with napkins and cutlery. Buying myself time. The truth was never easy, was it?

"I had a pretty small family, actually. And what about yours?" I asked, trying to deflect from myself as gently as I could manage it. "You said you used to have a big family?"

"My husband died about ten years ago. Bad heart. And then my daughter, who used to fill this house with people, took up with some man in Denver and I haven't seen her since. She always says she's going to drop in, but…" Calla's eyes crinkled in the way that they might when someone smiled, but her lips pressed into a thin, joyless smile that gave her away. "You know how it is. Folks got to make their own choices."

A mouthful of perfect scrambled eggs lodged themselves in the back of my throat. If anyone had cared enough about me, they might have been saying the same thing about me just a few days ago. *She took up with some man in Savannah, and we haven't seen her since.* Calla's eyes were sweet and sad when she continued.

"But you know, if she'd been here, then I might not have volunteered to look after the Bride House. And then we never would have met. So, there's a reason for everything, isn't there?"

"You have a very optimistic view of things, Mrs. Holtzman."

Optimistic was putting it lightly. I'd always been one to search for the sunny side of any situation, to power forward with the best attitude possible, but the way she was able to turn her apparent heartbreak into a new way to do good? It was almost otherworldly, how strong she must have been. She waved my reverence away, though, and sipped on her fresh cup of coffee.

"Call me Calla. Everyone else does. Now, we should probably talk logistics."

"Logistics?"

I'd already read her handbook. How many more logistics could there be? As she spoke, I turned back to my breakfast, forcing myself to not devour it as quickly as I wanted to.

"Yes. Now, you know the shape of the Settlement Initiative, I'm sure. Here for a year, job or small business loan, living stipend. Yes?"

"Mm-hm," I said, not wanting to talk with my mouth full of pancake but not willing to rush the perfect bite of breakfast.

"So, the first order of business is really simple. What do you want to do?"

She opened a notebook at her side, poising her pen in her left hand as she held up a freshly composed egg and sausage sandwich in her right. *What do you want to do*, she asked, as though the question were so simple. As though any of us really had a say in what happened. I shrugged.

"I hadn't really given it much thought."

"Not in your entire life?"

"I'm not really the dreamer type."

After all, dreaming was not for people like me. Surviving was.

"Well, we'll just have to try and find the dreamer inside of you. If you could be doing anything, right this very minute, what would it be?"

I raised my pancake-covered fork in a teasing toast. "Is professional breakfast eater a job?"

"Maybe somewhere else, but not here, unfortunately. Not yet, anyway. In the off-season, a lot of the restaurants close, so you wouldn't even have very many places to try right now even if there was. Come on. Dig deep. Dream job."

"Like I said. I'm not really the dreamer type."

That, I hoped, would be the end of it. And to my relief, it was. Did I have a dream? Yes. But a ridiculous one that I would probably never share with another human being as long as I lived.

"That's just fine, then," Calla said with a crinkle-eyed smile. "There are plenty of places in town that have created openings for anyone who joins our little Initiative. We'll just start you on one, and if it's not a good fit, then we'll move on to something else. How does that sound?"

Truth be told, it sounded like slow, unbearable torture. Even the thought of going outside of this house proved a strain on my mental defenses. In here, at least, I knew I was safe. But out there…?

"Are you sure I couldn't just work around the house? I'm handy with a paintbrush. I could help with the repairs around here. Or I could do all of the cleaning—"

"The point is to get you out into town, Virginia. To be part of our community. Hiding in this house wouldn't do much good now, would it?"

"No. Of course not."

This time, it was *her* turn to end the conversation. Finishing the last of her pancakes, she reached for a tote bag slung over the back of her chair.

"And to that end… I'm going to the farmers' market. Would you like to come?"

I glanced down at my pajama pants. "Right now?"

"What? Do you have a prior engagement?"

"No."

"Then, come on. We'll walk there and make room for all of the free samples."

After I'd slipped into more publicly acceptable clothes—the town of Fortune Springs might have been quirky, but I didn't think it was *wear your pajamas out of the house* quirky—Calla led me through the streets of town towards a small park, where several rows of booths had been set up for vendors of all kinds. For the next hour, Calla took her time, stopping at each booth, introducing me to the owners—who she knew by name—and helping herself to as many free samples as she could get her hands on. Tagging along, I tried to follow her lead. Smiling. Waving. Asking quiet questions here and there when I could think of something inoffensive and forgettable to say.

It certainly wasn't the maze of fear I'd been imagining when I'd been back in the house. No one approached me too suddenly. No one snuck up on me or tried anything that might cause me to jump. Not to mention that the atmosphere was as beautiful as it had been yesterday.

But somewhere between a blueberry cart and a stall selling freshly baked bread, I saw him again. Mr. Firefighter T-shirt himself, standing just in the next row of stalls down from us. I turned away quickly, hoping he hadn't seen me.

Calla didn't miss a thing. She raised an eyebrow in my direction. "You alright over there?"

"I shouldn't have eaten so much breakfast." I faked a smile as best I could. "I can't stop taking the free samples."

"It's a weakness of mine, too. But I really meant if you're alright being out here. You look a little bit concerned."

For a moment, I debated telling her the truth. But with the warmth of the breakfast we'd shared and the fun of this morning's adventure to the farmers' market, I couldn't force myself to lie.

"There's this guy I keep seeing," I confessed, lowering my voice as if he could hear me. "I met him yesterday, when I was trying to get directions to the house, and he wasn't exactly the friendliest to me. I just don't want to run into him again."

"Well, where is he?"

"Don't look, Calla!"

She waved my near-shriek away. "I'm an old woman. I'm allowed to stare. Where is he?"

"Like, my four o'clock."

Calla's eyes slid around the crowd, and then, she stopped. "Oh, that's just the fire chief. Owen Harris. A good kid. A little quiet. Reserved."

I almost snorted at that, and returned to examine the various animal-shaped bread loaves in front of me. "He wasn't quiet *or* reserved yesterday."

"Probably because he hates the Initiative."

"What?"

"He was our only real vocal opposition to the program. Thinks the money would be better put to use on the Fire House."

A note of bitterness entered Calla's tone, one that almost made me laugh. Right. Sure. *He's* the bad guy for wanting a town surrounded by mountains and supported by the logging of trees to have a proper fire department. I shrugged, noncommittal as I could manage. "Maybe he was right."

"If he'd been right, then you wouldn't be here right now. And that's not a trade I'm willing to make. I'm going to go talk to him."

Panic struck me, hard between the eyes.

"No—"

"Not about you, silly girl. He and I aren't necessarily on good terms, but sometimes he sends me guys from his fire station to help out with little projects around the house. Real neighborly. We've got a leak and it's supposed to rain tonight, so I want to ask him about it. Why don't you come with me? I'll properly introduce you."

The panic gripped around my throat now. The edges of my vision went fuzzy. "Oh, no thank you."

"He's not as scary as he looks. Really, he's a big teddy bear underneath that gruff exterior. Hey, Owen! Get over here."

Oh, now she was bringing him over *here*? No, I couldn't... I couldn't do that.

"Why don't you give me the groceries and I'll take them home?"

"I don't—"

But before she could refuse, I'd already turned on my heel and begun rushing back to the house.

Chapter Four

If Calla was upset with me for abandoning her at the farmers' market, she was good enough not to mention it. Instead, when she returned home with the last of her purchases, she swanned in through the living room—where I'd been looking through a tall stack of secondhand books, waiting to be slipped into the empty bookshelves—and invited me to help her unpack.

The rest of the day passed in companionable silence on my part and nonstop talking on Calla's. She carefully danced around the subject of Owen Harris, but mentioned that someone would be coming to fix the leak in the ceiling later on, and I could feel free to make myself scarce around seven to avoid them if I wanted, before practically skipping onto her next topic. As I sat at the kitchen counter, leafing idly through packets of potential jobs, the afternoon slipped away from us as she began preparations on something that looked like cherry cobbler.

It was there, and then, sitting at the counter, that I realized I really liked Calla. A dangerous prospect, considering I'd be gone from this place in a year, but true all the same. She was a mess of contradictions—kind and firm, rough and soft, welcoming and protective—but each of those contradictions, somehow, only made her more likable.

Thankfully, she had clearly decided to go easy on me for today and she didn't ask me any more about myself or my life up till now, or my hopes for being here in Fortune Springs. She was content to talk, and I was content to listen.

At least, until the phone rang. All day, as the hours ticked from morning to afternoon the weather had been gathering overhead, and by the time the shrill sound echoed through the house, making me jump, the clouds had begun filling the house with gray-streaked light. Putting aside her pie prep, Calla raced to the phone, leaving me alone in the kitchen to listen from afar.

It wasn't eavesdropping. Could it really be called eavesdropping when the person you overheard spoke loud enough for the entire town to hear?

"Yes, hello?" she crowed, her voice reverberating through the wood-floored hallways.

Silence. A sharp intake of breath. Then, the solid walls of Calla's tone broke into a concerned, frayed mess. Every few words, she would stop, then try to rush out some more, then repeat the whole process. With every word she spoke aloud, her words from earlier today reverberated in the back of my mind. *My daughter took up with some man in Denver and I haven't seen her since.*

"Oh, baby. Please—slow down. Oh… okay. I can come and get Willa. Just… Where are you? Okay. Bring her to your neighbor's house. Make sure she stays there. I'll be there soon. I love you."

With that, she slammed the phone back down on the receiver, hanging up and ending the call.

Before I could so much as wrap my head around what I'd just heard, Calla raced back into the kitchen, her hands blindly reaching for the coat on the hook next to the back door. Her nervous energy permeated the air, agitating every inch of my being. Over the last few years, I'd become attuned to peoples' emotions and restructuring my life around accommodating them. With Calla in this state, I turned to helper mode.

"What's the matter? Is everything okay?"

The sleeves of her coat weren't cooperating, so while she struggled with the fabric, I collected her keys and oversized coffee mug. The whole day I'd never seen her go anywhere—not to the farmers' market, not to another room in this house—without it. "My daughter needs me to look after my granddaughter. She's in Denver. I'm going to go there now and pick her up."

Without another word, Calla took the keys and mug from my hand and started for the front of the house. A woman on a mission. I followed behind at a close clip. Overstepping boundaries was not something I wanted to do, but I couldn't help but offer what little help I could.

Calla had brought me here. Given me a place to try and start over. The least I could do was be helpful when she was clearly upset and under a hell of a lot of stress. From what I could piece together from Calla's frantic, broken phone call and her current mood, her daughter's deadbeat boyfriend had done something to spook the mother, prompting her to call and beg her own mother to rescue the child in the scenario. If anyone wanted to help in a situation like that one, it was me.

"Do you want me to go with you?"

"No, I think she might need some time alone with me. The car ride might do her some good. But can you—"

A stricken look passed over Calla's face. She halted the process of buttoning her coat. "Do you think you'd be able to let the repair guy in? I'd call and tell him to come another time, but the leak is only going to get worse—"

"I can handle it."

I said it without thinking or even mentally confirming with myself that it was true.

"You're sure?"

"Yes," I said, again without thinking it through. I knew that Calla would waste time trying to make me comfortable, and that was time she didn't have. Not right now. "Absolutely. Go."

"Thank you. Thank you, Virginia."

As soon as she left, the house seemed darker. The creaks in the floorboards louder. The rain swirling outside of the window, threatening an upcoming storm, seemed more violent. Walking into the living room, I pulled a blanket off of an old, beat-up antique chaise longue and wrapped it tightly around my shoulders, reminding myself over and over again that it was just the rain. Just the rain. And my brain playing tricks on me.

I stayed there in the living room, watching the front driveway, for too long. From the corner of my eye, I kept track of the clock, shooting my gaze from it to the front yard and then back again.

Every so often, the creeping anxiety of the empty house would crawl up the back of my neck and nestle at the base of my skull. The groan of a pipe awakened goosebumps all over my body. My heart jumped into my throat at the sound of a creaking floorboard. And I had to repeat the same thought over and over again.

There isn't anyone here. You're okay. You're free. You're safe. You're safe. You're safe.

Seven o'clock rolled around. The television crackled with the same mindless TV show that had been playing a marathon all afternoon. Then five minutes passed. Ten. Fifteen. A false hope swelled in my heart. Maybe the repairman wouldn't show. Maybe I wouldn't have to be in this house with a strange man. Maybe—

Thunk. Thunk. Thunk.

I jumped, the sound of three solid collisions of knuckles against wood breaking me out of my hopeful spiral. The sound, though, didn't come from the front door. I'd had my eyes on the front steps almost the whole time; no one could have gotten there without me seeing. Jumping from the couch, I made my way through the kitchen to the back of the house. It had started raining some time ago, and the anxious *thwick, thwack* of the droplets against the roof underscored my anxiety.

That's when I saw him. Almost like a mirage through the hazy pane, Owen Harris stood on the back step. His shoulders firmly set in a mirror of the grim line of his lips.

Stopping a few steps short of the door, my socks almost slipping against the tile, I stared at him for a long moment. Glancing down at the phone in his hands, he seemed completely unaware of my existence, giving me an opportunity to safely scour him visually. He was even more intimidating now, with his clothes slicked to his hard body by the rain and his hair hanging loosely over his eyes. With the barrier of the window between us and the light and rain playing off of the pane, I couldn't make out the color of those eyes, but I could see the smooth lines of his face wrinkled and tightened by some emotion I couldn't quite identify.

My own emotions weren't exactly easy to identify either. There was certainly fear, the same fear I felt any time someone got too close, the same fear I felt any time an unpredictable element entered into my life. But there was something else too. A tightness in the pit of my stomach that didn't come from the fear; a feeling that almost reminded me of being at the top of a rollercoaster—all anticipation. It gave me a faint, reassuring buzz, one that assured me I could be brave.

I threw open the door before I could lose my nerve. The last thing I wanted was to tell Calla I'd been too afraid—or too *something*—to do the one thing she'd asked of me.

For a second, unencumbered by any divisions between us, he looked up from his phone and stared at me, his jaw slightly parted.

"You're not Calla."

"Good eye."

Tension twisted between us, like the air just before a crash of thunder. Despite the fact that he knew I lived here, he was clearly as surprised to see me here as I was to see him.

"I'm…" he started, but apparently thought better of whatever he was going to say and offered me a firm nod in its place. "Hello."

"Hi."

Another lull of silence. This time, less tense and more awkward. His expression slowly sunk from surprise into something more harsh, more closed-off and contained. It wasn't anger, not exactly. But it was something decidedly unpleasant. Annoyance? Frustration?

Truth be told, I was feeling a little of that myself.

"What are you doing here?" I asked, my voice choking at the back of my throat.

"I'm here to look at the leak."

"I mean, at the back door."

He shrugged, pulling the wet hem of his T-shirt higher up on his hips. "More trees on the backstreet. Helped with the rain."

Oddly, there was something comforting about this gruff man and his clear dislike of me. In my experience, men with ulterior motives, men who you were supposed to fear, started out by laying on the charm nice and thick. Lulling you into a false sense of security before striking. This guy…? He couldn't charm a banana out of its peel.

Shifting my weight from one foot to the other, I tried to tell that to my hand, which held on painfully tight to the doorframe.

"I thought someone else was coming."

He raised an eyebrow. Maybe he wasn't charming, but he was handsome, even when annoyed. "Someone else?"

"Someone…" *Someone else? Someone who might actually be nice to me? Someone who wouldn't make me feel like standing my ground and running for the hills all at once.* When none of that seemed right, I just nodded to his general person. "Not you."

Something flashed in his eyes. Pride? "I've got two working arms and a toolset. What's wrong with me?"

"You don't seem to like this house very much. Or me, for that matter."

Another shrug. This time, I was smart enough not to follow the trail of his wet T-shirt as it traveled up his stomach. I kept my eyes focused on his, which pointedly avoided my gaze. "No one else was available tonight. Calla said it was urgent, so I decided to come over myself instead of asking her to reschedule. Is that okay with you?"

It wasn't so much a question, but a challenge. One I wasn't going to back down from. I hadn't traveled halfway across the country and totally restarted my life to go back to cowering now. No matter how much I might have wanted to.

"Yeah. Sure."

Another silence. It wasn't until he spoke again, this time with a bit of wry humor, that I realized I still hadn't moved from my spot blocking the doorway.

"Can I see to the leak now?"

"Go ahead. It's—"

"She told me where it is."

And just like that, he took a step forward and I immediately retreated, letting him slide past me and into the house beyond. Not wanting to lose sight of him for safety reasons—I didn't want anyone sneaking up on me—I followed behind at a close clip until he hovered beneath the site of the leak, which was currently dumping into a giant, rusted pail on the hardwood floor. He inspected it, then turned, turning those disarming eyes squarely on me.

"Ladder?"

"I've just moved in. I don't know where the ladders are kept."

"No, you're standing in front of the door. The ladder is in there."

Oh. Right. Quickly—but not too quickly, considering I didn't want him to "win" whatever unspoken contest we were competing in—I stepped aside and watched from the opposite wall as he pulled and unfolded a ladder from the utility closet beneath the stairs. Despite Calla's insistence that he didn't like the Bride House, he seemed to know his way around here pretty well.

As he put himself to work, pulling down a vent from the wall above, and leaning into the ceiling to fiddle with pipes I couldn't see from the floor, I distracted myself from the sight of his too-tight jeans spreading across his ass and the sound of the strengthening storm outside by worrying about how I would clean up the mess of him once he left. If Calla had been worried about the leak, she would definitely have been worried about the constant drip, drip, drip of Owen Harris' clothes onto her floors.

"Did you walk here?"

He grunted as he adjusted a pipe, but the sound almost came out like a laugh. "What gave it away?"

"All the puddles I'm going to have to mop up once you leave were my first clue."

"It's a small town. I walk almost everywhere unless I need to put out a fire."

"Even in the rain?"

"Yes. Even in the rain."

His voice was tightly controlled, as if he was struggling to hold back some emotion he didn't want me to hear in those five simple words. My mind traveled back to Calla's words today at the farmers' market. She'd said he wasn't as bad as he looked, implied that he was basically a big softie. I didn't see it. There wasn't a soft thing about him. But the fact that Calla—a person I had decided *I* trusted—seemed to trust *him* really dug under my skin and nestled there uncomfortably. What did Calla see that I didn't see?

Or, maybe more to the point, how was it that he could be civil to Calla, but went out of his way to dismiss me at every turn?

After a long stretch of consideration—and tightening my arms across my chest as though that could keep the words bottled up inside—I practically barked up at him. "Have I done something to you?"

"Besides being here?" With the steady drip, drip, drip of the leak finally halted, he continued to speak as he made his way down the ladder. "They might have given the fire department the funds if no one had showed up to claim the Bride House money, you know."

"Oh, I'm sorry," I said, unable to bite back the mouthful of sarcasm. I hadn't known that about the Bride House and the money they were using to fund the settlement program, but still. I couldn't believe it was wrong to be here, just like I couldn't believe he was genuinely upset at me for it. "If I'd have known I was putting you out, I definitely wouldn't have traveled halfway across the country on a bus. I hate to be an inconvenience."

SMASH! Just at that moment, the entire house flooded with the white-hot light of lightning and the wall-shuddering crash of ever-closer thunder. My anger snapped, only to be replaced by a shriek and a cry of terror that flew out of my mouth before I could stop myself.

Even worse, I'd jumped nearly out of my skin... and right into Owen's strong, surprisingly gentle embrace. My heart racing, my breath coming out in small pants of fear, my chest rising and falling against his touch... it all fell away as I looked up into his large, understanding eyes. Gone was the harshness of his expression. Everything was soft. Solid. Almost kind. "It's thunder," he said, softly. He made no move to push me away or shake off my embarrassing display of fear. A minute ago, he couldn't have cared less about me. After all, I was the one who'd ruined his dreams of a new Fire House and a town without strange women in it. But now, he held me like he genuinely wanted to protect me. "It's only the storm."

This was the first time I'd been touched this tenderly by a man since… Well, I couldn't remember the last time a man had treated me like this. Especially one who didn't seem to care about me twenty seconds ago.

Almost as fast as I had jumped in, I jumped out of his arms and turned away, busying myself with the stacks of junk mail on a nearby end table. It wasn't much of a plan, ignoring him and hoping he would leave without another word. But the thought of looking him in the eye right now filled me with a kind of deep, lingering uncertainty. I didn't know if I had the strength to face it.

When he realized I wasn't going to say anything else—or acknowledge his existence, even—he cleared his throat.

"The… the leak's fixed."

"Thank you."

"I'll be going now. Tell Calla to call me if she needs anything else."

And just like that, he was gone. Despite the storm, he left from the front door this time, apparently more eager to escape from me than he was worried about getting wet. For too long, I stood in the long hallway, stuck in place as I tried to process what had just happened. A strange man came into my house—how strange to already think of it as "mine"—gruffly brushed me aside and showed his annoyance at me being here at all, but comforted me when I was afraid of the storm, only to immediately seem embarrassed about having done so.

It was too many emotions to process at once. Too much to handle. Awhile back, I would have buried my feelings with fake smiles and gone about my business, but tonight, with the storm raging all around the house, cloistering me inside, I chose a different route. One I never would have considered even a week ago. I went into the kitchen, collected the candy jar from the bottom shelf of the pantry, and immediately returned to the living room, where I turned on the gaudiest reality TV show I could find. And for what felt like the next few hours, I let the wine throwing on the screen and the sugar high from the Tootsie Rolls just carry me away.

I didn't know how long I'd been sitting there or how many episodes of junk TV I'd consumed by the time the front door swung open.

"Alright, we're home," a voice straining cheer chirped from the entryway.

Collecting myself from the couch, I headed towards her.

"Calla—"

But my feet stopped short, just in the frame of the living room, when I caught sight of the both of them. Calla, the woman who'd seemed ageless as the statue of a conquering warrior queen, seemed as if she'd aged ten years since the last time I saw her. Clothes and hair matted to her body, she'd clearly given her raincoat to the young lady standing timidly at her side, her face a blank, void mask. She held tight to a single suitcase, clinging to it the way only yesterday I'd clung to my backpack. As if it held everything she owned in this world.

"Oh, Virginia," Calla said, clearly trying to put on a good show of warmth and normalcy for the girl at her side. "I'm glad you're still up. I want you to meet my granddaughter, Willa. She's going to be staying with us for awhile. Willa, this is Virginia. She's new in town, too."

"Hi, Willa," I said, trying a smile of my own.

"Hi," came the small response.

In this little girl, I saw a mirror of myself. Scared, alone, but too proud to let any of that show. The last thing I would have wanted in her position—the last thing I had wanted when I'd shown up here and met Calla for the first time—was pity. So, instead, I just held out the candy jar to her.

"You look hungry. Candy?"

Willa didn't answer right away. Instead, she glanced up at her grandmother, as if for permission. Calla nodded. "Go ahead."

Almost as soon as the words were out of her mouth, Willa's hand dove in, and pulled out a fistful of pre-wrapped candy. She shoved the pieces in her pocket quickly. Another tactic I recognized—hoarding, just in case someone tried to take back what they'd just given to you.

As she set about hiding her treats, I turned to focus on Calla who, with her granddaughter preoccupied elsewhere, had finally let her steely-smiling exterior slip. Now, I turned the candy jar on her. A small gesture. But it was all I had at the moment.

"What about you, Grandma? You look like you could use the sugar rush, too."

Chapter Five

That night, my sleep wasn't nearly as good as the first night I'd spent in the Bride House. For one thing, my skin kept recalling the feeling of Owen's arms around me. For another thing, before bed, Calla had informed me I'd be starting my first day of work at a local diner after the weekend, a fact that filled me with enough anxiety to stave off sleep for years.

And for another thing, the little girl who'd just joined our house? She spent the entire night crying herself into lulls of quiet sleep, waking up for more tears, and then repeating the process all over again.

I knew the feeling. I didn't know the specifics of what had happened to her, just the generalities, and still, I knew exactly what she'd been through. What she was *going* through.

The one thing people never tell you about starting over? How hard it actually is. Sure, you think it'll be great to reclaim your life and stake out your independence and live out your fresh, new, clean existence. But once you do, then you have to face down lonely nights in a strange house. The reality of leaving behind everything you've ever known before.

You have to face the knowledge that everything you went through before was wrong. That you wasted time and energy and love on something so broken you needed to rescue yourself from it.

It had been hard enough, trying that at twenty-seven. I couldn't imagine doing it at twelve. My heart broke for her.

And it was a combination of all these factors that caused me to tread lightly over the next few days. She was just as new as I was, and I followed Calla's lead in not pushing her too far beyond eating meals with us or watching TV in the late afternoons as we discussed my first upcoming job here in town. Every so often, she would let slip some errant thought or piece of conversation before retreating back into her shell, and I could tell she was starting to, slowly but surely, settle into life here just as I was.

Then, on the third day of Willa's time with us—my first day at my new job here in town, as it happened—Calla apparently decided that the comfortable stasis we'd all reached was no longer acceptable.

"Virginia, there you are! I was about to run upstairs and get you. Do you think you could do me a favor?"

"If you keep making breakfast like this, then I think I could do just about anything you ask, Calla."

"It's about Willa."

The serious tone told me I'd better listen up. So, I did just that. After what I'd seen the night of her arrival and what I'd heard through the walls of the house as I tried to sleep, it wouldn't take much convincing to get me to help her.

"Oh?"

"I need to run down to the school to get her registered. It's pretty late in the year still, but I think it'll be good for her to have some structure and stability, you know? Make some friends. Get to be part of the community here. I don't know how long she'll stay, but I want her to feel like she can for as long as she wants, you understand?"

"Of course."

"Well, I'm going to need to talk to Principal Hernandez about..." Calla's expression strained. There was no delicate way to say, *I'm going to need to explain to her principal that she's come from a broken home and will need some extra care and attention*, so she danced around it as best she could. "Well, I've just got to talk to him about getting Willa into that school of his. I already called Bette down at the diner, and she said Willa could take a book and sit in a booth today while you work. Would that be alright with you?"

Oh. When I'd heard *a favor for Willa*, I'd thought maybe picking her up some healthy snacks for the house or helping her find her way home from school. I hadn't thought about having to keep an eye on her all day. Not that I minded it, of course. It's just... what if I said the wrong thing? What if I *did* the wrong thing? She was already in a tough enough spot as it was. I didn't want to make things worse.

"Calla, I don't know. Don't you think she'd be better off with you—"

"Please. She just needs a friend. Not a grandmother right now."

About an hour later, I found myself on the short walk from the Bride House to the restaurant where I'd be starting my first shift. Nerves abounded inside of me, not just because of the prospect of a new job, but because of Willa, walking at my side.

I'd made such a mess of my own life. What if I screwed hers up as well?

Still, it felt wrong to look out for her all day while simultane-ously ignoring her, so I cleared my throat and attempted to strike up a conversation. Everyone liked self-deprecating humor, right? "You know, I haven't ever waited tables, so this will probably be a disaster. You're going to have plenty to tell Calla about tonight at dinner, I bet."

No answer. Willa merely held a large, hardback book to her chest a little tighter. Her eyes remained squarely on the sidewalk ahead of her.

"Pretty big book you've got there," I said, trying a different approach. Her bookmark peeked out from near the front of the book, so I tried another joke. "Think it'll last you until the end of the day?"

Either my jokes weren't very funny or she wasn't into conversa-tion. Or both.

"Not much of a talker, huh?" When she didn't respond, I shrugged. I completely understood why she wouldn't want to talk to anyone, especially a stranger. I knew the feeling. "That's alright. I'm usually not such a big talker, either."

That awakened a reaction from her. "Really?"

"Yeah, I know you'd never believe it, hearing me now, but I'm usually pretty quiet. Don't like to draw too much attention to myself. But you know, if you want me to do the talking for a little bit, I don't mind."

"Did my grandmother put you up to this?"

"No," I assured her. The truth was more complicated. The truth was that I knew exactly how it felt to walk in her shoes, and I wasn't going to let her feel as lonely as I'd once felt. "We women have just got to stick together, that's all. Even when things are hard. *Especially* when things are hard."

Our walk carried us down to The Mountaintop Retreat, the diner that was neither on a mountaintop or much of a retreat here on the main road through town. I stopped us in front of it, shot a look down at my much shorter companion, and raised a conspiratorial eyebrow. Maybe I couldn't hold myself together very well in this new life I was trying to build for myself, but I could at least try and help *her* through this. "Now, come on. You want to go inside and see me be the world's worst waitress?"

It took a moment of indecision, but eventually, the ghost of a smile tugged at Willa's pale, tired face. I winked, braver than I felt and hoping she didn't notice.

"Yeah, that's what I thought. Let's go."

I'd been joking when I'd said I would make the world's worst waitress. Like everyone else who'd never done food service work before, I'd vastly underestimated just how difficult the task would be.

But even worse? I'd vastly overestimated myself. And my own strength.

Turns out, I wasn't half as strong as I'd thought I was. Because every time someone moved behind me, or caught me by surprise, or crossed the corner of my vision too quickly, my performance from the thunderstorm gave an encore, and whatever I'd been holding in my hands—a full pot of coffee, a plate of dirty dishes—went crashing to the floor.

By the time my shift ticked into its last hour, I'd repeated this three times, and had to go through the motions of cleaning everything with the eyes of the diner upon me.

My boss, Bette Romero, a sweet woman with sharp eyes and a wheelchair in serious need of some WD-40, was trying her best not to fire me on the spot. I could tell that every time she pointed over her shoulder to where the mop and bucket were kept behind the counter. Willa, though, was a sweet kid. She'd shoot me sympathetic looks, then laugh when I rolled my eyes at my own clumsiness. At least, that's what I hoped people saw it as. Clumsiness, and not the latent strains of fear tugging constantly on the back of my mind.

The Mountaintop Retreat was typical of a small-town American diner, but instead of being stuck in the 1950s, with black and white flooring or jukeboxes, this place was decorated with chalet coloring and wood—a cozy place to grab a cup of coffee or a big, greasy omelet before hitting the slopes or the trails for the day. Now, long after the morning rush, when most of the men working up on the mountain's logging operation were already on their way to work and there wasn't a tourist in sight, the place was neither bustling nor a ghost town. An easy flow of folks came and went, lazily taking their time through their coffee and pancakes before leaving for the rest of their day.

Thankfully. Considering how badly I'd been doing so far. Now, my only two tables were tucked away in the back corner of the place, right near Willa so I could keep an eye on her. This, I could handle. Quiet folks quietly sipping their coffee, waiting for their breakfast. No one to sneak up on me. No one to shock my system. I could handle this. I could handle this. I could—

"Hey—"

Then, with a plate of discarded breakfast plates high over my head balanced precariously on a tray, a voice—deep, rumbling, dangerous and promising as thunder—awakened every one of my senses. Without fully giving my body permission to do so, I spun towards the source, wanting to have it in my eyeline. I already knew who it belonged to, already dreaded seeing him here. But when I turned, I realized we were too close for me to do any seeing at all.

Our bodies collided.

"Oh!"

The tray—along with my entire body—went crashing down to the tiled floor as I bounced off the firm, solid body of Owen Harris. It all happened so fast that by the time I finally looked up at him from my fallen position, I realized that only a second had really passed between us. His jaw hung limp. Was that…? Was that concern I saw in his eyes? Worry? Or, stranger still, regret?

"I'm so sorry. I'll get you—"

"*You!*"

The word came out more accusation than shocked gasp, a fact that I regretted almost immediately, when his dark eyes narrowed in response.

His jaw dropped. "What do you mean, *you?*"

"What are you doing here?" I asked, hating the way I wanted to wilt under his direct stare. Forcing myself away from him, I focused on carefully collecting the broken plates from the floor and mopping up the spills from the plastic cups as well as I could manage with the already-wet rag at my hip.

"Getting breakfast. What are *you* doing here? Besides destroying all of the dishes, of course."

"Forget it. Bette's going to be—"

So mad at me, was the way I'd intended to end that sentence. An intention he crushed when he cut me off with a question of his own.

"What are *you* doing here?"

"I work here."

"Since when?"

Snapping at him would have been very easy then. But when he slowly moved down to my level, crouching so he could collect a few stray shards of shattered plate, a note of gallows' humor entered my tone. Bitter and laughing at the universe all at once.

"Since about four dropped platters ago. Maybe two hours. This is my first job in town. Part of the Initiative, you know. Oh, maybe you don't. Because you hate the Initiative. And me, apparently."

His hand stilled over a cup, which had rolled towards his feet. His voice faltered slightly, a fact that I tucked away for later study. "You think I don't like you?"

"What else am I supposed to think?"

He reached for the tray, suddenly determined to look anywhere *but* at me. "I can help you—"

"It's fine. I don't need your help."

That sentence had an unspoken coda to it: *Not like you helped me last time I saw you.* Apparently, he heard it without me having to say it, as his entire form stiffened in response.

But if I'd hoped blowing him off would keep me from drawing attention to myself, I had another thing coming. A shrill voice entered the main dining room, accompanied by the squeaking of a slightly rusty wheelchair.

"What happened here?"

I jumped to my feet, the tray clattering with its broken wares. "I'm sorry, Bette—"

Again, before I could finish my planned thought, Owen interjected yet again, in that commanding, but not *demanding* voice of his. He flashed a charming grin, too, the kind of grin that usually made women swoon on the spot.

"It was my fault. I wasn't paying attention and I just bodied her trying to get into my usual booth."

"And you were the one who made her trip the other three times today?" Bette asked, the lines in her face deepening with disapproval.

"Not physically, but probably in spirit. You know, she's seen me around town before, Mrs. Bette. I was probably just on her mind, distracting her."

"I can't believe I still let you come in this place, when you talk and say things like that."

"You know you love me. And you love Virginia here, I bet. She's been doing a great job."

"A great job of breaking all of my dishes."

A moment of apparent indecision passed through the air as Bette sized me up. For my part, I stood completely still and silent, banking on the vain hope that if I didn't move, maybe Bette wouldn't see me. After a moment of silence, she pursed her lips in an accommodating smile that practically screamed *thanks, but no thanks.*

"Listen, Virginia. Your shift is about to end. Why don't you go ahead and bunk off early? Get your head on straight. You're new in town. I'm sure this is all very overwhelming and I'm just not sure this is the job for you."

It was an arrow, straight to my heart. Failure. Just like I'd always worried. That in my new life, I'd be nothing but a failure. My bottom lip started to quiver. Heat built up behind my eyes. But I forced a smile and waved over to Willa's booth.

"Yes. Uh, yes, m'am. Willa? Come on. Let's go home."

A moment later, we were outside, ready to head back to the Bride House with my head hung low. This time, I was grateful for Willa's speechlessness. I wasn't in the mood for talking anyway. All I wanted was to retreat back home and bury my head under the covers for a few hours. But it couldn't be that simple. Oh, no. Not with Owen Harris, Resident White Knight and Bride House Hater in town.

"Wait a second! Hey!"

He'd followed us out, and was now following us down the sidewalk. With a small nod towards Willa that she should walk ahead, I straightened my shoulders, gathered my courage, and turned to face him.

"Yes?"

His eyebrows knit together in something approaching concern. "Are you okay? Bette's not usually like that."

I still couldn't get a read on him. One minute, he hated me and wanted to keep me at arm's-length, the next, he was trying to stop my boss from firing me. It didn't make any sense. Just like the feelings welling up inside me weren't making any sense—a mixture of excitement and trepidation.

"Why did you try to help me back there? I didn't ask for that," I said.

"I think the words you're looking for are *thank you*. As in, thank you for fixing the leak in my house and thank you for protecting me from the big, bad thunder and thank you for trying to help me keep my job."

The reminder of the incident during the rainstorm made the hairs on the back of my neck rise. "Yeah, well, you didn't, did you? I lost my job because of you."

That's wasn't a fair characterization of what had just happened, but right now, I didn't care. My ego was bruised, my feet were killing me, and I was too sticky from constantly cleaning up syrup to worry if I was being fair to him at all.

"I had good intentions," he said, his voice a little bit softer now.

"I can't keep my place at the Bride House on good intentions. Unless…" A light bulb went off in the back of my head. It was a leap, to be sure, but still, it made sense, given the way he'd been acting since our first meeting. "Unless that's your plan. Get under my skin and run me out of town so you can take back the program's money."

"I'm not doing that. Listen, I think you and I got off on the wrong foot." Clearing his throat, he extended his hand for me to shake. I did not take it. I wouldn't take anything from him. "I'm Owen Harris. I'm the fire chief here, and if you need anything—"

"Don't worry. I won't."

Chapter Six

Over my first few days at the Bride House, I'd begun to learn the little quirks and unspoken languages of the woman in charge of it. At first, I'd thought Calla to be unreadable—a mixed bag of tiny gestures and teasing tones and frontier gruffness.

My opinion had changed over our short time together, though, especially once she'd rushed to bring her granddaughter to the safe haven of this house. And when I walked through the front door after my terrible first day at work, still shaken from my latest encounter with Owen Harris, there wasn't much room for interpretation in Calla's expression.

The woman lingered in the front entryway, near the corded, black telephone that hung to the front wall, as if she'd only just hung it up. The cool air blowing up from the brass vents in the floor ruffled the hem of her gown and carried the scent of her perfume—and her disappointment—straight to me.

First, she opened her arms to Willa and tucked her into a hug. Then, she turned her attention to me, let out a withering, hurricane-force sigh, and only said, "I don't think candy's going to do the job on this one. Let's all go get a drink."

By drink, of course, she meant a cup of tea in the kitchen, but given the exhausted, *already at the end of her rope* defeat with which she said those words, she might as well have poured all three of us—including the child—shots of whiskey and called it a day. I didn't even drink, but every time I thought about the smashing of dishes and omelets against the black and white marbled floor of the diner, I wanted nothing more than to get silently drunk and stay that way for a good and long time.

For awhile we all drank our tea in silence. It didn't last.

"Do you want to talk about it?" Calla asked.

"Do *you* want to talk about it?" I replied, turning the tables. It was clear that things hadn't exactly gone well so far today for either of us. And it wasn't even noon. My first day at work had been nothing short of a disaster and, apparently, her trying to get Willa enrolled late at school hadn't gone much better.

Calla glanced at her granddaughter from over the rim of her teacup. "Principal Hernandez is worried about distractions this close to the end of the school year."

Even with the sticky-sweet syrup covering what felt like half of my body, goosebumps erupted all over my skin. A flash of righteous rage flared through me.

"She's a kid, not a distraction."

"That's what I told him. But he's not sold." Turning to her granddaughter, she gave her hand a squeeze. "Don't worry. We'll figure something out. Now, it's your turn."

That last directive was for me. I almost groaned. I'd rather do another shift at the diner than recount my disaster of a morning.

"Do I have to?"

That was a genuine question, not a rhetorical one. Calla was a hard woman to pin down. Sometimes, she seemed content to wink and let me keep my secrets. She'd never demanded the details of what I was hiding from, for example. But other times, she put her foot down and demanded answers.

In this case, I was pretty sure Calla already knew the answer. She'd been tipped off about the disastrous shift at the diner before Willa and I had even walked through the door.

"I wouldn't have asked if I wasn't really giving you the choice," Calla muttered, over the rim of her coffee mug.

"I mean, you've obviously already heard about it."

A shrug. "Word travels fast in a small town. Especially when you're something of a celebrity."

Calla nudged my shoulder, apparently trying to make a lighthearted joke out of my current situation. When I merely shared a glance with Willa, her grandmother decided more explanation was required.

"I'm friends with Bette, who owns the joint. I thought it would be a good starter job for you, something that might ease you into the town a bit, make you new friends. But—"

"But I blew it."

That's what this was really all about, wasn't it? I'd been given such a simple job and I couldn't even handle it. I'd underestimated just how skittish I was. Even the relative safety of the restaurant—where I knew, realistically, that no one could hurt me—I spooked too easily, immediately dropping my tray and ruining not only the plates but the mornings of the customers who depended on me.

I knew it wasn't the end of the world. Logically. But logic sometimes wasn't powerful enough to stop the gnawing in the pit of my gut, the deep, male voice in the back of my mind reminding me over and over again that I was a failure. That this was a stupid idea. That I should just go back to Georgia because I'd never be able to make it on my own.

And to add insult to injury, my humiliations couldn't even be private. I'd made a fool of myself in front of the townsfolk at the diner, in front of Willa, in front of Owen Harris, and now, I was recounting my shame to Calla.

She winced, trying to put the truth as delicately as possible. "You didn't make the world's best impression."

"I really *was* trying. I just have trouble with people. With crowds. It's hard for me, but really, I can do better. I *will* do better—"

For what felt like the thousandth time today, I was cut off. This time, though, it was from a most unexpected source.

"But it wasn't her fault!" Willa said, almost breathless as she looked up from her cup of tea.

Calla looked as shocked at the declaration as I felt. She blinked several times, as if waiting for a mirage to dissipate, and when it didn't, she leaned forward.

"What was that, dear?"

Willa gulped, but gamely continued. "Fire Chief Harris was there. I remember him from when I was a kid. He made her drop the last tray and *that's* why she got fired. It wasn't her fault at all. It was really *his* fault."

"Owen Harris?"

The note of quiet excitement in Calla's voice—paired with the light flooding her eyes—didn't fill me with joy. Quite the opposite. My stomach plummeted. I hadn't been planning to tell her about the Owen Harris part of it all. They'd looked pretty chummy at the Farmers' Market.

"Yeah," I said, shrugging it off. "I keep running into him. Fixed the leak a few days ago and then he was at the diner this morning."

Willa interjected once again. This time, her eyes had the same twinkling excitement that her grandmother's held. "He likes her."

That prompted a laugh out of me. "No, he definitely doesn't."

I recounted the whole story, then, leaving out only a few crucial details. Calla didn't need to know how handsome I found him, and how dangerous I found that attraction. I wasn't here to feel anything for any man. I was here to get my fresh start and get the hell out of here once my contracted year in Fortune Springs was up.

Willa, of course, interjected her two cents every once in awhile, adding ridiculous punctuations about how Owen's eyes looked longingly into mine, something that had, in fact, never happened.

When I finished the slightly abridged versions of my encounters with Owen, I waited patiently for the verdict from Calla. When waiting took too long, I added a question. My own anxiety from my earlier conversation hadn't subsided. The fear nettled me.

"Do you think he's trying to run me out of town, Calla? Do you think that's why he's getting under my skin like this?"

"No, he wouldn't do that. He's not the type."

Her answer was immediate, dismissive. A ripple of shock passed through me. How could she be so sure of something like that? Sure, maybe he didn't seem the type on the surface, but people were capable of anything when pushed hard enough. I knew that firsthand.

"Are you sure? Because it really seems like—"

"I promise, dear. He may not like the Bride House, but he wouldn't ever do something to intentionally hurt anyone. He likes to save people, not destroy them."

For a long moment, I gazed at Calla, searching her face for any hint of doubt or second-guessing. I didn't find it. Instead, I only found profound belief in a man who left me guessing at every turn.

In that moment, I was faced with a decision I'd been faced with a half-dozen times since coming here to the Bride House. I could either run, or I could trust Calla. And like every other time before, I put my faith in her.

"So," I asked, "what do you think *is* happening here?"

"Well. After your little story, I think everything's starting to make sense to me. It's all coming together now."

I blinked. One of the things I didn't love so much about Calla was her tendency to speak in riddles. "What is?"

"Owen Harris talks a big game, but he isn't anything to be afraid of. He's gentle as a kitten, really."

"Really?"

Once again, there was that unshakable belief in him. She nodded, only once, to punctuate that belief. "Really. He's quiet, and introverted. A bit of a loner. But if he's taken to you—"

"He isn't."

Right? He wasn't *taking to me*. Sure, he'd protected me from the "big, bad thunder," as he'd called it. And then, there was this morning, when it'd been clear he'd wanted to help me out of a tight spot at the diner. But taking to me? Not a chance.

"Well, it just seems to me that if Owen Harris, noted cynic and opponent of the Bride House, took a shine to its first recipient, then maybe he won't be such a tough nut to crack after all."

"I'm not sure I love the way you're looking at me right now, Calla."

"Maybe…" *Just hear me out* hung in the air, unspoken. "Maybe if our resident fire chief learned to like *you*, he could learn to like the Bride House. And the program. If we could turn our most vocal opponent into our most vocal supporter, if we could convert *him*, then maybe we could silence all of those quiet naysayers and doubters for good."

"And how do you suppose we manage that?"

I had a feeling about what she was going to say next. A feeling I wouldn't like it.

"Well, you'll have to spend time with him, of course. It's not easy to avoid a man like that in this town. And if the two of you meet and things just *happen* to go well between you… then maybe that wouldn't be such a terrible thing, would it?"

The lilt in her voice told me that it was more of a desperate wish than a casual suggestion, so I tried my damnedest to slightly steer the subject in a different direction.

"Maybe I should focus on keeping a job before I focus on finding a man. And maybe we should *all* focus on getting this one," I nudged Willa, who gamely stuck out her tongue at me, "into school before we focus on anything else."

But Calla only smirked and winked, and even from this distance, I could practically hear the wheels in her head turning. "We're women, dear. We are the masters of multitasking."

Chapter Seven

"This is all your fault, you know."

I adored Willa. And in her, I saw something of a twelve-year-old kindred spirit. A kid who needed protecting and help even when I couldn't protect or help myself. She was also, in my opinion, a dirty rotten snitch who'd gotten me entangled in a mess of Calla's making.

As Calla handed me a fresh-baked tray of brownies—swirled with caramel and peanut butter; the fire chief's favorite—I stuck out my tongue in Willa's direction, earning me a small reciprocal gesture in return.

"Oh, hush, you," Calla said, waving my concerns off. "This is going to be great. You go over there, bring him the brownies as *my* thank you for fixing the leak here in the house, and who knows? Maybe you two will patch things up."

The possibility of *patching things up* with Owen seemed remote at best, but I held my tongue. Destroying Calla's hopes of reconciliation didn't seem very fair. I tried to turn her attention to the kid instead, only half-joking.

"Why don't you send Willa to do it? People go nuts about kids doing cute stuff like this. Or you? You're very cute. Maybe he'd like it better if it came from you."

"Well, thank you, my dear, but I'd like to think I know Owen Harris better than you. Trust me. He'll want these to come from a beautiful woman."

I snorted. I owned a mirror. I'd heard people talk about me. I knew exactly what I looked like. Frizzy red hair. A generous heaping of freckles. Hips too wide and shoulders too broad. I'd heard plenty of times how unattractive I was, how lucky a break it was that I got any attention at all. "Let me know if you find one."

As Calla led me to the front door, I couldn't see her face, but I watched as her shoulders tensed. There was no mistaking the distance in her voice, either. "Someone hurt you real bad, didn't they?"

"What makes you say that?"

"That's the only reason I can figure why a woman who looks like you is saying something that foolish. That's all."

With that, she opened the door, and Willa joined at her side to see me off. My voice lodged uncomfortably in the top of my throat. She implied that I was beautiful, that the only reason I didn't know it was because someone had told me otherwise.

Those invisible strands tethering me to my old life tugged. The sensation wasn't pleasant. The only way to escape it was, well, escape. Literally. I could either stay here in this discomfort, or find a new discomfort down at the Fire House.

"Wish me luck." Calla did so, but before I slipped out of the house, I teasingly narrowed my eyes in Willa's direction and whispered, "Traitor."

*

It was impossible to miss the Fire House in a town like Fortune Springs. The Engine House on State Street must have been one of the highlights of any tour around Fortune Springs, at least from the outside. I wasn't sure what it looked like on the inside, of course, but on the outside she shone. White-painted letters across the front of the gray and red-accented facade declared it ENGINE HOUSE NUMBER ONE. Considering I'd never seen an Engine House Number Two, I figured it must have been built in one of the town's more optimistic moods, when everyone believed that one day, Fortune Springs would be big enough to sustain multiple engine houses.

The main thing about the Engine House, at least from my vantage point out front, was that it looked well-loved. Well-taken care of. Sure, it clearly needed repairs—repairs that, after the Settlement Initiative, they couldn't afford—but someone really loved this place. Enough to keep it in as good a condition as possible, given the circumstances.

I wondered if that person was Owen. According to Calla, he lived here in an apartment above the station. Was he the one who meticulously manicured the grass and cleaned the windows? Were his big, strong hands the ones that kept the lights on in the front window and the curtains drawn upstairs?

It only took one step up onto the creaking board porch for me to immediately regret coming. I had nothing to say to this man, no experience talking to people like him. Calla's harebrained scheme to get us into a state of detente seemed particularly far-fetched. For a moment, I considered running to the nearest park, devouring the entire tray of brownies myself, and hightailing it back to

Calla's with the empty tinfoil. But I knew I couldn't do that to her, no matter how much I wanted to. A new plan formed in the old one's place. I rang the doorbell, making a split-second decision to leave the brownies on the welcome mat and run home as fast as I possibly could.

But as fast as I possibly could wasn't fast enough. Because before I'd even managed to bend down, the door swung open, revealing the one person who made me freeze and want to run all at the same time.

How was it possible that his eyes were that arresting? That the strange swirl of emotion in them could transfix me like this? I told myself that it was because this time, he was different than he had been before. His usually primly combed hair stood in riotous waves; dark circles painted half-moons beneath his eyes. He looked… unwell. Worse than he'd ever been in any of our previous encounters. His lips slipped into an almost self-deprecating smirk.

Even the smirk looked tired. Almost forced. But I got the sense he wasn't forcing it because of anything I'd done, but something else. Something that had happened long before I'd arrived. I didn't usually trust my own instincts, but in this, I felt almost certain.

"We've got to stop meeting like this."

"Are you okay?"

The words were out before I could stop them. I'd been told before that this was one of my worst traits—I wasn't capable of ignoring suffering. I'd done plenty of it in my life, and no matter who was affected, even someone like Owen, I didn't know how to turn my back on it. He fell back half a step, as if the simple question were an arrow instead of a harmless collection of words.

"Me?"

"I don't see anyone else around here."

If I'd been surprised by his concern at the diner yesterday, this time, he took on the same role. Rubbing his eyes with the heels of his hands, he seemed almost convinced that he could wipe away my interest just as easily.

"Sorry, you've just seemed... very disinterested in me since we met. The concern surprises me."

"I guess I'm as disinterested in you as you are in me," I said, my mind flashing back to our first few encounters, the ones that left me in the center of a sea of conflicting emotions. "But still. Are you... are you okay?"

"Yeah, I just haven't been sleeping very well lately. Lots on my mind."

Intrigued, I raised an eyebrow, silently prodding for more information without consciously giving myself permission to do so. An arrogant thought entered my mind, a selfish one. Had he been thinking about me? Had he been kept awake by our handful of brief encounters?

"My dog's been having some trouble, I think. Nothing to worry about, though, hopefully."

That didn't sound like the whole truth, but the admission seemed like a big one coming from him, so I let it go, offering him the tray of brownies as a means of distraction.

"Calla wanted me to bring these over. To say thank you for fixing the leak."

His eyes lit up with all the glee of a kid on Halloween. The exhaustion previously shadowing the lines of his face dissipated. "Caramel?"

"And peanut butter."

"She knows me. Thank you for bringing them over."

"No worries. Bye."

The hand-off complete, I flashed my most courteous smile and turned to make my way back to the Bride House. I knew I should feel nothing but relief at putting my back to the fire station and the man who ran it, but the closer I got to the front gate, the colder the air seemed to be.

Strange. I'd been ready to run out of here the second I arrived. Why now, all of a sudden, did I want to stay?

"Wait."

And even worse, why did my heart give a small flutter when his voice reached out to me across the yard, calling me back to him?

"I'm really sorry. About the way I've made you feel. About getting you fired yesterday. About everything, really."

Sorry. I couldn't remember the last time I'd heard a man use those words, much less mean them. And he did mean them. For the first time, I understood what Calla saw in him. There was a dependable honesty in his words, a ring of truth that could not be faked, not convincingly anyway. My heart skipped again, making my voice break halfway through my reply.

"It's—it's okay."

"No, it isn't. What I did was wrong, and I'm sorry. I'm not very good with people, you see."

A wry chuckle escaped my lips as the events of my first few days in Fortune Springs came rolling back to me. "Yeah. Believe me. I see it."

As soon as those words were out of my mouth, I tensed for the inevitable backlash, for the anger that usually came when I let my words run away from me in front of other people. But instead, he surprised me. He laughed, too. And when the laughter died out, it didn't disappear from his lips or his eyes.

"Do you..." I watched as he visibly swallowed. "Do you want to come in? I can't eat this whole tray of brownies on my own. Or, I guess I *could*. And I probably will if you don't have one. But I definitely *shouldn't*, if you know what I mean."

"I don't know—"

Despite what I knew about him now—that he wasn't the monster I'd thought him over the last few days, that maybe Calla was right about him after all—panic rose up the back of my neck, hot and splotchy. Again, in a surprise move, Owen sensed my discomfort without me having to say it out loud. He raised his hands and his eyebrows in a show of surrender.

"Or we could stay out here, if you want. I know it can be kind of weird to go into some strange guy's house. Maybe we could start over. Pretend that the last few days didn't happen."

"You know, I think I'd like that."

And to my surprise, that was actually true. After these last few minutes, after knowing how much Calla trusted him, after feeling the strange surge of warmth that filled me when he smiled his crooked, sincere smile at me, I *did* want to start over with him.

Closing the gap between us, I walked up to the porch, where he'd settled the brownies on the porch swing, and took his extended hand to shake.

"I'm Fire Chief Owen Harris. Nice to meet you."

"Virginia Bessel. It's nice to meet you, too."

We held hands for a moment too long. Or maybe I held his hand too long and he was just too polite to pull away. His grip was strong and soft at the same time, as perfect around my palm as it had been around my body during the thunderstorm. When, finally, I realized how long we'd been standing there, I pulled away with a small, embarrassed cough.

"Let me run in and cut these," he said, diffusing the tension by reaching for the brownies. "I'll be right back. Do you want a drink? A coffee or a milk or anything?"

"A coffee would be great. Just enough milk to change the color."

"You've got it."

He disappeared into the house, but left the door open so I could hear his rustling around inside. Leaning against the doorframe, I breathed in the air from inside the Fire House, letting it wash over me. This wasn't a male scent like the last one I'd been accustomed to. All sweat and whiskey and dirt. This was clean. Wood and ash and coffee. Instead of setting me on edge, it actually relaxed me.

That's when I realized I'd smelled it before. When I was in Owen's arms.

Soon, the house filled with the sounds of a coffee grinder preparing fresh beans for brewing.

But there was something else, too. Something smaller, just beneath that sound of blades against coffee pods. A whimper. A sound of distress.

"Hey, Owen? Owen?"

He didn't hear me. The sound pulled me in closer to the door. So close I hadn't realized I'd actually crossed the threshold and entered the Fire House.

There it was again. The sound of a creature. A creature in pain. I called out to Owen again. But there wasn't any response but the sound of his humming and the coffee grinder working away.

I weighed my fear of entering this house, alone with Owen, against the thought of an animal in distress. It wasn't any contest.

Without stopping to think twice, I started up the Fire House staircase.

Chapter Eight

As I moved my way up the stairs, the sounds of the coffee being made down on the first floor fell into the background while the whimpering slipped into the foreground. Creaking floorboards beneath my feet accompanied the sound of the animal, which I followed up, up, up the rickety stairway, into a small, humble apartment, and finally, into a bedroom.

It was a simple space. A bed, a dresser, a television set flanked by DVD box sets of *Battlestar Galactica* and *The West Wing*. Interesting TV choices, which I filed away for later contemplation. An old flannel shirt hung over the radiator in the corner, rumpled and apparently drying off in the heat from the machinery below and the streaming sunlight above. The bedside table held a small collection of books with the spines turned away from me, and a flyer advertising the local school's career festival.

But none of that caught my eye. Not really. Instead, I focused on the source of the whimpering, of the sound that had driven me away from the porch and all the way up here.

A long, beautiful Dalmatian curled up beneath the radiator, looking as pitiful and heartbreaking as it was possible for an animal to look. All other thoughts flew from my mind at the sight of her.

Carefully, I approached and moved to my knees, holding out a hand for the animal to sniff before I moved any closer.

"Hey, girl. What's your name?"

The dog took two sniffs of my fingers, gave them a small lick, and retired her head back to the bed currently tucked up beneath the radiator. Taking that as an acceptance of my presence here—or at least an admission that the pup was too exhausted to do anything about it—I reached out to check the dangling, bone-shaped tag on the red collar around her neck. One side was etched with the address of the Fire House. The other, the dog's name.

"Polka." Like polka dot. Clever. "That's beautiful."

Another whimper. Polka's eyes widened, then slipped closed. Her breathing was at turns erratic and wild, then shallow and steady. My assessment from the bottom of the stairs hadn't been wrong, then. The animal was in distress.

Gently, I reached out to stroke Polka's soft ears, letting the waterfall of fur run beneath my fingers. I'd been around enough dogs in my life to know that the sudden arrival of a stranger—or the introduction of a horrible sound, like a coffee grinder—could turn even the bravest pup into a cowering, uncertain mess.

I knew the feeling. If I'd had the option to cuddle up in a nice, warm bed beneath a radiator instead of venturing out of the Bride House, I probably would have taken it in a heartbeat.

"Oh, you poor thing. You don't feel so good?"

Leaving the ear scratches behind, my hand moved down to stroke Polka's flanks. But the moment I reached her shoulder blades, my fingers tensed.

"You're cold. Is that… Is that normal?"

No, it wasn't normal, and I knew that almost as certainly as I knew Polka wasn't suddenly going to start responding to all of my queries. Having grown up on a farm, I knew a lot of things about animals that most people probably didn't. Like how to clean out a horse's hooves or that mice hate lavender.

Or how to tell that a dog is about to go into labor.

No time to waste, then. Despite the fact that I'd been a city girl for a while now, the years of looking after the animals on my family farm suddenly kicked in. Instinct and training took over. Get Polka comfortable. Get her warm. And let nature take care of the rest.

Completely ignoring the fact that I was in a stranger's house and that this was a stranger's dog, I set to work, ripping a blanket off of the nearby bed and wrapping Polka into it.

"Here. Let's get you all tucked in."

To my surprise, I didn't panic at this strange twist in events. Sure, a million questions raced through my mind—How many puppies would there be? Did Owen even know that puppies were on their way? Would *I* have to tell him? How was I going to do that?—but they all faded into the background as I did everything I could to make Polka comfortable. All my errant thoughts and worries and anxieties dissolved under the weight of this new imperative.

Help Polka bring new life into this world.

But, of course, a few minutes later, my serene path suddenly and sharply turned right—straight into the waiting arms of Owen Harris.

"Polka, come here, girl—"

The man himself entered the room, apparently oblivious to my presence and when he stopped squarely in the doorframe at the sight of me, he promptly dropped the bowl of dog kibble to the floor.

Polka didn't even flinch at the food rolling around so close to her. She whined again.

In any other version of this scenario, I would have shot to my feet, apologized immediately, and run out in embarrassment. I would have ducked my head and left as quickly as I possibly could without falling over myself.

But considering Polka yowled every time I took my hands away from the soft folds of her neck, I couldn't do any of that. My number one priority right now was not my own pride or the shock in Owen Harris' stunning eyes. My number one priority was seeing Polka and her puppies safely through this delivery.

My mouth did hang open, though. Owen's did too. "I…"

"What are you doing in my bedroom?" he finally spluttered, more surprised than unkind.

"I was just…" *Come on, Virginia. Hold it together. Don't melt just because you're cornered in a room with this guy. Stay strong for Polka. You've got to.* Squaring my shoulders, I cleared my throat and tried to do just that. "I was downstairs and I heard whimpering and I thought something might be wrong. I think that something *is* wrong."

"And what is that?"

"Well, actually, I guess it depends on your definition of wrong. It's just that I think you're about to get some new residents of this Fire House."

I shot him what I hoped was a meaningful look. Thankfully, he took the hint.

"You think she's—"

"I think we're about to welcome some new puppies."

Maybe it wasn't fair to drop such a sudden bombshell on him like that. Plenty of people didn't realize when their pets were pregnant. But in that moment, I watched with keen interest as the strongest man in the entire town—this stoic, brutal, blistering mountain of a man—suddenly crumpled into a pool of shameless, unbound anxiety and terror.

I guess it was true what they said about dogs being man's best friend.

"But I'm not—she can't be… Oh, Polka, you're—Is she going to be okay?"

"Are you going to be okay?"

He didn't look it. Gripping the doorframe as if he was worried he'd collapse without it, his face went sheet-white and ashen. His eyes widened and focused on the dog as though there was nothing else in the room to see.

I wasn't sure what to make of that. A man who would, at turns, face down a stranger because he didn't want her in his town, then turn around and try to make amends with her, *then* break down at the mere thought of his dog being in pain. I'd never known a man like that before. All I knew was that, for the first time in a long time, I found myself alone in a room with a strange man and I wasn't afraid.

Using his one free hand, Owen ran his fingers through his mane of blond hair. Every muscle in his body tensed; he moved with the jerky energy of an anxious wind-up toy soldier. "The only veterinarian is in the next town over. I don't know if we have enough time—"

"I'm sure she'll be fine."

Men and childbirth. I'd never believed the rumors of their freak-outs until now, when I had front seats to one.

"You should go," he spluttered. "I'm sorry that you got caught up in all of this."

For a moment, I considered the offer as I continued to rub at Polka's flanks. He was as good as giving me an out, absolving me of any responsibilities to stay here. If I was smarter, maybe I would have run downstairs, back to the Bride House, and pretended none of this ever happened.

But between the whimpering dog whose cries shook my hands and the staggering man in the doorway who couldn't seem to catch his breath, I knew I couldn't turn my back on this. Maybe he wanted me gone. Maybe this was his way of politely telling me to butt out of his affairs. I could understand that. But I could tell that as helpful as he probably was to the folks in this town, he was going to be useless here and now. Not just to Polka, but to himself.

"No. I don't think you should be left alone. Either of you. And I have a little bit of experience in this area. I'm not leaving poor Polka here alone."

"She won't be alone."

A small laugh tripped, unbidden, over my lips. "She will be if you pass out. Where are your towels? And where can I get a basin of some warm water? And a heating pad, if you have it."

"I'll get it all. Does she need her toys? Or treats? Are you sure I shouldn't call the vet? She might be able to drive down here in time—"

There it was again. The freak-out. Giving him what I hoped was my most understanding, nurse-like look, I shook my head.

"Polka is going to be fine."

He didn't look convinced. But he also didn't look *unconvinced* either. Just… deeply and supremely worried. When he spoke again, though, he only said, "She's my best friend."

"And I'll make sure I take very good care of her. I grew up on a farm, so I've helped bring my fair share of puppies into the world."

Again, I laughed. Not because anything I'd said was particularly funny, but because I wanted nothing more than to wipe that twisted angst from his handsome face. When that didn't work, when he didn't even try to take part in my laughter or lift his lips in a smile, I offered, "Let's just say that we're even now. You apologized for getting me fired, and now, I'm returning the favor by helping you with Polka."

"You don't need to return the favor. It was nothing."

Well, I'd succeeded in one respect. He was no longer anxious over the dog. Now, he was sheepish and looking everywhere *but* in my direction. I wasn't sure if I could call that progress, but it was a start, at least.

"It wasn't nothing. Not to me."

He looked down at me. And I looked up at him. There was a moment then. No, not a lowercase moment. But A Moment. The kind I sometimes saw people have in movies, where all of the sparks played out invisibly across the camera, reminding the audience that there were big things on the horizon for these people.

I didn't want to feel those sparks, much less imagine that anyone else could see them if they happened to catch sight of this moment.

But there was no denying that they were there, fogging up my vision and filling up my chest with champagne bubbles.

Eventually, Owen cleared his throat, shattering whatever might have just passed between us—had it only been my imagination?—and he stuck his thumb over his shoulder, pointing towards something I couldn't see.

"I'll just go get that stuff, then."

"Thank you."

And just like that, just as quickly as he'd appeared, he vanished. Just like all the other times he'd popped into my life, he left me with more questions than answers, more feelings than facts.

I couldn't remember the last time feeling something for a man didn't strike me with panic. I didn't know what that meant... and I wasn't so sure I *wanted* to know, either. Leaning down to press my cheek against Polka, letting the soft fur bring me back down to Earth, I checked the animal's temperature and muttered against her ears: "He's not such a bad guy, is he, Polka?"

This time, as if she could understand, Polka didn't whimper or cry out. Instead, her tail gave the slightest, most sincere wag. I smiled. "No, I don't think so either."

Half an hour later, with the heating pads and blankets and water and myriad of other supplies firmly set into place, Polka let out a sharp, harsh *yowl* that could only mean one thing.

"It's starting now."

One look at Owen's face granted me a glimpse of his suddenly green complexion. His lips pressed together in the way you might if you were trying desperately not to throw up. "I don't think I can watch," he protested, as much as he could without opening those lips too far.

"Okay," I replied, doing my best to keep calm for all of them. "Close your eyes, then. Just scratch her ears. Tell her it will be okay. Make her feel safe."

Make her feel as safe as you made me feel that night in the thunderstorm.

For a moment, Owen hesitated. But soon, he lowered himself down to her level and did as he was told, muttering the words against the soft fur of the animal's ears.

"Alright, Polka. It's going to be okay. It's going to be okay…"

Soon, the sound of Owen's voice softened the tense muscles in Polka's body. I tried to ignore how reassuring *I* found his voice, too.

Chapter Nine

An hour or so later, I almost couldn't remember what it was like to be close to this man and feel afraid. At first, I'd been too distracted by the impending puppy birth to care about him being so close. Now, with mother and puppies all safely accounted for and healthy, I realized I didn't care anymore about having no defenses against him.

The puppies and their mother weren't the only ones safe here. I felt like maybe I was, too.

As Polka snoozed soundly in her bed, her soft snores dancing lightly above the sounds of the house—washing machine running, air conditioning whirring—I tried hard to focus my attention on the four snoozing puppies tucked into various parts of my body. One rested on my right thigh, one on my left. A twin set nuzzled into the crooks of my cradling arms. I didn't want to dwell on the comfort I felt here, how easy it was now that the wall between us had completely collapsed.

I also didn't want to dwell on how sweet he looked across the room from me, cradling two puppies in his arms as though they were the most precious creatures to ever walk the earth.

"This sure was a hell of an introduction," he muttered.

"Hm?"

"Remember? I said we were going to start over? If this was the way we'd *really* met for the first time, it would have been really something, wouldn't it? Thanks for helping me. I wouldn't have known what to do."

"Don't mention it," I said. "Anyway, I hope you really like dogs."

A hesitation punctuated his words. "I do."

"I'm sensing there's a *but* in there somewhere."

He focused his attention on the puppies in his arms. I watched as tender compassion filled his expression. "I always thought animals were a very practical thing, you know. Some people get animals to help with the ranching work or to guard their fence lines or to get rid of the rats in their barn. I love Polka, but I got her because, you know, it's the thing to do when you live in a Fire House. But this…"

"This is something different, isn't it?" I knew what he meant. "They're the most beautiful little creatures *I've* ever seen, anyway."

"You really like dogs, don't you?"

I nodded, but wasn't going to get too into it. How did you tell someone that growing up, dogs were your only friends? You didn't, not unless you wanted to sound pathetic. "More than just about anything."

"So, you're a waitress, your name is Virginia, and you love dogs. That would make one hell of a dating profile."

The conversation was light, almost teasing. I couldn't help tuning in. Without my conscious permission, my lips turned up in a smile.

"Don't you start, too. I'm getting enough of that dating talk from Calla."

"You don't want to get out there? Play the field? It's a small field, admittedly, but isn't that one of the reasons you came here—"

I couldn't answer that question without giving myself away. "Besides, I'm not a waitress anymore, remember?"

He raised a curious eyebrow. "In the market for a new job?"

"Something like that. I'm sure Calla will have something new lined up for me once I'm finished licking my wounds. Or cleaning up all of the syrup I managed to spill over myself during my time at The Mountaintop Retreat."

He considered that for a moment, as if rolling through a mental help-wanted list. "Well, I hear they're hiring down at Gold Teeth Pete's. It's a local saloon. Might be fun."

My stomach turned. The ghost of whiskey-scented breath filled my nose. No. I wasn't going to be working at any bar. Not any time soon, anyway.

"Oh, no thank you. Not my thing."

"Mine either."

That, like many of the turns this evening had taken, surprised me.

"Seems like a waste in a small town like this," I said, trying to fish for information without making it obvious. "During the off-season, there doesn't seem to be much else to do."

My line came up empty as Owen returned my jab with a jokingly affronted retort. "Hey! I'll have you know that Fortune Springs has a rich and vibrant social scene. There's so much to do around here."

"Like what?"

One of the puppies sneezed in his arms, the smallest and sweetest *achoo* I'd ever heard. Owen's jaw dropped, then closed again as he tried to think of anything, culturally speaking, to recommend in this little town. "Well, nothing's coming to mind right now, but I'm sure I'll think of something."

"And I'm sure these little guys will keep you busy," I said, nodding towards the pups, who managed to nestle deeper into my embrace, if that was at all possible.

"They seem to like you."

I shrugged, as best I could while balancing so many little creatures. "I'm a dog person. I always wanted—"

Before the thought could resolve itself, I cut it short, holding back the truth I'd almost let slip. I couldn't tell him *that*. I'd only told one other person that crazy dream, and they'd laughed in my face at the ridiculousness of it all. Owen didn't let me get away so easily, though.

"Always what?"

"It's stupid. Forget it."

The small smile he'd been sporting spread into an incorrigible grin that did things to my heartbeat I wasn't entirely comfortable acknowledging. "Oh, don't leave me hanging like that. You've got to tell me."

Telling him the truth of my one, big, impossible dream was *so* not going to happen. Just because I trusted him enough to stay here, alone with him, for a few hours didn't mean that I was comfortable telling him that. "No, really. You'd lose any respect you might have for me. It's just… such an impossible dream. One of those things you know you're never going to get, so you might as well never talk about it."

"Those are the best kinds of dreams," Owen replied.

"Not in my experience," I answered.

The sound was wistful and regretful all at the same time. That was the tightrope I walked now, wasn't it? I carried my regret like a reliable suitcase, knowing I'd never be able to put it down, all while waiting for the train that might take me towards a better future.

Careful not to disturb his own handful of pups, Owen leaned into me, his eyes sparkling as he did so. "I promise I won't tell a soul. I can even give you an embarrassing daydream of my own, if you want."

I forced my gaze away from him, and reached out a fingertip to stroke one of the puppies on my thigh with an easy, light finger. Maybe the softness of the new babe would distract me from the softness in Owen's features. "Yeah?"

He replied without even stopping to consider whether or not it was a good idea. He spoke with gusto, the kind a kid might employ while giving a lecture to his fourth-grade class on career day. "I always dreamed that one day, I would play quarterback for the Denver Broncos."

"Why didn't you?"

He barked out a laugh. The sound was so caramel-sweet it almost made me want to laugh along. "Right. You're new in town, so you've never seen the annual Thanksgiving Firefighters versus Town Council Flag Football game. I couldn't become a player for the Denver Broncos because of my utter and complete lack of talent in everything regarding the game of football. Besides watching it, of course. I've always been pretty good at that."

"I find that hard to believe, you're so—"

Once again, I stopped myself from revealing too much, too soon. Heat flooded my face, and I was sure by now that I was blushing.

"I'm so what?"

We shared a look from under my thick curtain of eyelashes. There were so many words I could use to finish that sentence. He was so *large*, for one thing. So strong. So athletic. But one word escaped my lips before any of the others, and I knew it was the one I really meant, deep down. "Intimidating."

"It's hard to look intimidating when you're holding puppies."

"True, but… still. I wouldn't want to cross you."

I tried to make it a joke, but it was one of those jokes with the ring of truth to it. Guilt knotted my stomach. I didn't want him to think I was afraid of him. Or that he'd done anything to *make* me afraid of him. Eventually, he offered a light smile that slightly lifted the mood.

"I don't think you ever could cross me. Besides, I'm not the kind of man who *gets* crossed. It's not in my nature. Not usually, anyway. But you're changing the subject."

"Which is?"

"Your dream. The one you're trying to avoid telling me about."

I scoffed and tried to change the subject, but it turned out I hadn't gotten much better at it in the few minutes since my last attempt. "I barely know you. It's a big thing to tell someone I've just met."

"I told you my secret. Come on. It's humiliating to have no hand-eye coordination and dreams of playing football at the same time."

Another pause. Memories flashed in the corners of my mind. Harsh laughter. Eye-rolls. *You'd never be smart enough to pull it off. You think anyone would want something like that, then you're crazier than I thought. Just stick with me, baby, and I'll take care of you.*

But then, I looked back up at him. Waiting for me expectantly. Hopefully. And I decided to trust him. It was a big decision for me, one that might come back to bite me in the ass later, but still. I made it.

"I know it's going to sound—"

"It's going to sound great. You don't have to qualify it for me."

That last part, offered lightly and calmly, made the decision for me. Sure, maybe my idea was crazy, but what wasn't? Hell, everything about my current situation probably sounded crazy. A stranger from a strange place moving into some place called the Bride House. Helping a misanthrope fire chief bring his dog's puppies into the world. But it was all true. It was all happening. Before I could think better of it, I forced the words out.

"I wanted to start a dog therapy program."

"Do dogs need therapy?"

"They don't—" I started to explain, but then saw the laughter lurking at the corner of his lips. He was teasing. "You said you weren't going to make fun of me!"

"I'm not," he chuckled. "I'm not. I promise. I think it's… I think it's a great idea."

"Really?"

"Yeah, really. Nothing makes me feel better than coming home and cuddling up on the couch with Polka."

"I wanted to get this big van and fix it up, so that I could offer animal therapy sessions to people and communities who needed it. Families in shelters and college students stressed out about exams and people waiting for their court appearances or—"

This time, it was habit, rather than nerves, that cut me off. Back in my old life, any time I got too excited, especially about this, it was only a matter of time before someone else shut me down. Now,

I did it to myself before anyone else could. Rolling my shoulders back, I tried to be cool once again.

"I don't know. I just think there's something beautiful about the power of connecting with nature. The way a puppy's little snoot or breaths can make you feel like everything could be okay. I was actually going to write a *very serious* research dissertation on it at one point."

"Sounds great."

"It would have been, if I'd actually finished school."

I don't know what possessed me to say that part out loud. Not finishing school was one of those failures I carried around my neck like a millstone. The decision to drop out had seemed so simple, once upon a time. Now, not having a degree just made me feel inferior to anyone else who'd managed to get that flimsy piece of paper.

"How far away from graduating were you?" he asked, not unkindly.

"Almost there. Just had to finish writing the dissertation."

"And you don't want to be a waitress?"

"Or a skiing instructor or a snowboard waxer or a receptionist at the timber yard or any of the other jobs Calla has suggested." As soon as I spoke, I wanted to take it back. "I mean, not that I'm ungrateful or anything, I swear. It's amazing that so many people have offered me jobs and all, but it's just not—"

"It's just not your dream."

There it was again. That one, loaded word. A single syllable with a million implications for which I could never answer. I guessed that some people in this life got the luxury of dreaming, but I wasn't one of them. Dreaming only led to disappointment.

"Yeah. My wild, impossible, never-gonna-happen dream."

"Well… I've got a litter of puppies. And there's a community college here in town."

My breath caught in my throat, so it took me a minute before I could muster a reply. "What are you saying?"

"I'm saying your dream is less of a moonshot and more of a walk around the corner."

Oh. He wanted to give me the puppies. He wanted me to take the puppies, get a degree, and have this one, small part of the universe I'd been secretly hoping for for most of my life. My reaction was immediate, almost sharp.

"I couldn't do that."

"Why not? You're here. You've got puppies. I'm sure we could find you a van somewhere. And a lot of people in this town could use a good puppy cuddle."

Strangely, that was something I'd noticed about the town, too. It didn't have the warm and cozy qualities that a lot of other small towns seemed to have in the movies. Everyone here was kind, of course, in their own way. But there was a frontier ruggedness about them. A skepticism and uncertainty and individualistic quality that everyone seemed to carry around like a shield.

Owen included.

But maybe that could change. Maybe if everyone could cuddle some puppies and talk about their feelings for a few minutes, maybe this whole town could open up wide.

"It couldn't be that easy," I muttered, mostly to myself.

"Why not?"

"Because nothing's ever easy in my life."

Maybe it was his close proximity. Maybe it was the small patch of common ground we'd found together. Maybe it was just the come down from the adrenaline of birthing several small animals, but I was being more honest than usual tonight. I rushed to correct my bitterness. "Sorry. That sounded so self-pitying. I just mean… Someone once told me that it was a stupid dream. Impossible. It seems strange that I could just… make it happen, you know?"

"Calla always said she wanted the Bride House to be a place for fresh starts. This one could be yours."

My fingers brushed against one of the puppies in my lap. Hope was so dangerous, but… it was also so close. I didn't know if I had the strength to deny it. "You'd let me have the puppies?"

"They seem to like you more than me anyway."

"I don't know what to say."

"You don't have to say anything. It's the least I could do after losing you your job."

I shook my head. I didn't want him to feel like he owed me anything. "You didn't lose me my job."

"Well, the way I see it, you helped bring the puppies into the world. It's only fair that you have them. If you want them, that is."

That dangerous hope and my own self-doubt warred inside of me. The voice of the man I'd left behind in my old life muttered that I would never be able to do it. That I would be a failure if I even tried. But still… I couldn't say no. Not just yet.

"Can I have a few days to think about it?"

Chapter Ten

When I got home that day from Owen's house, I went straight up to my room and stayed there, completely ignoring all of Calla's questions and cries from downstairs. I needed time to think. Time to plan. Time to measure and weigh what I actually wanted.

By the next day though, I still hadn't figured it out. Not entirely. The experiences of the last few years of my life told me to run away as far and as fast as I could go. That I would be too stupid, too weak, too small to ever figure out anything like a business on my own. I still wanted this dream, yes. But was I really brave enough to go out and get it?

I didn't know. I wasn't sure I'd *ever* know. And when I descended the stairs for breakfast and found only an overflowing pile of food on the kitchen counter and Willa reading through what looked like the world's largest book, I was still chewing it over. Thankful for the distraction from my thoughts, I turned my focus to her as I fixed myself a plate of farmers' market pastries.

"Heya, Willa."

"Hi, Virginia," the short, brown-braided girl said, her voice quiet and careful as ever.

"What are you doing over there? That looks like a pretty big book."

"Well…" There was a pause, as if she was weighing what to say next, or *if* she should say anything at all. "Grandmother told me that she's not sure when I'll be able to go back to school, but I didn't want to fall behind. So, I went to the library yesterday and checked out some things to keep me on track."

"You really want to go back to school, don't you?"

"I like school. I'm good at it."

A fire lit beneath my skin. School was a distraction for her. She needed it. I could understand that. And just because I couldn't get my own life back in order didn't mean I was completely useless. The flyer in Owen's bedroom, the one advertising the local school's career festival, stuck in my memory like a bookmark, and I knew what I had to do.

Little Willa was going to get into that school if it was the last thing I did.

Was I distracting myself from my own troubles by focusing on hers? Yes. Absolutely. But did I care? No. She was a child and she deserved to go to school, and so help me, no one was going to label her a distraction and be done with her. Not on my watch.

"Alright. We're going to get this figured out."

"What do you mean?"

"I mean we're going to get you into that school if it's the last thing we do, okay?"

"Grandmother says she's been working on it—"

"I'm sure she has, but that doesn't mean we can't try a few tricks of our own."

*

I'd always thought it was easy to get lost in a crowd. Safety in numbers. That it was much easier to blend into a large group than it was to disappear when walking by yourself.

But when Willa and I walked into the gymnasium of the Helen Hunt Jackson County High School that night, any hope I might have had in our blending in vanished on the spot. It was evening now, and parents and students alike lingered around coffee stations and tables propped up by local trade unions and universities. Chatter, which I'd heard from several feet outside the door before we'd even walked in, seemed to slow and quiet at our entrance. Eyes followed us.

We were the town oddities. The first Bride House girl and eccentric Calla's granddaughter from out of town who arrived under mysterious circumstances.

Every muscle in my body wanted to turn tail and run. The last thing I'd wanted when I'd come to Fortune Springs was any kind of attention or notoriety. I'd wanted peace and quiet, tranquility as much as invisibility, and being here was setting my hope for all of those things aflame.

But when I looked down at Willa, I knew I couldn't run. There was so much excitement in her eyes. Her small hands, wrapped around a new pile of books we'd collected from the library on our walk over here, practically shook with the thrill of being around so many children her own age, of teachers guiding students around display tables, of the promise of learning.

Her words from this morning echoed in my ears, louder than any noise echoing in this gym. *I like school. I'm good at it.* Even the unspoken part of that refrain came back to me. *School is a good distraction. School is safe.*

So, against every instinct I'd built up over the last few years and over the objections of every one of my fears, I lifted my chin, straightened my shoulders, and marched directly into the fray. Past strangers with slightly slackened jaws, past wandering eyes and curious whispers. I wouldn't show any of the fear I felt. Not to them, and certainly not in front of Willa.

Instinct told me to find a woman with a clipboard. Women with clipboards always held the power at events like this. Scanning the crowd, I searched until I found a slight woman with a tall bun, a chain attached to either end of her spectacles, and a big button declaring her name to be MRS. WHITLOW!! I went straight for her.

"Hi. Good evening, Mrs. Whitlow," I said, making a big show of inspecting her shiny, marker-decorated button. "I was hoping to talk to Principal Hernandez."

The woman shifted from her left foot to her right; her nervous eyes followed a similar pattern. "And, uh, who are you?"

I knew full well that this woman knew *exactly* who I was. By now, everyone in town probably knew what I looked like and all of my pertinent details. Gossip traveled fast in a small town, if Calla's direct line to everything that happened around here was any indication. Still, I extended my hand and a smile.

"I'm Virginia Bessel. I just moved into the Bride House. We're here to get Willa here enrolled in school," I said, with a finality I hoped signaled the end of any argument.

"And you're her… mother? Guardian?"

"Family friend."

A wash of relief colored the pale woman's skin. Apparently, she thought she'd just been given an out to conflict. "Well, unfortunately, we're in the middle of an event right now, so the principal is very busy, as I'm sure you can imagine. And seeing as you're not her parent or legal guardian, I'm afraid you couldn't get her signed up for school anyway—"

That flash of hot rage, an echo of my anger from this morning when Willa told me how badly she wanted to go back to school, erupted beneath my skin, and I lifted my chin defiantly. But before I could even attempt to get out a protest, a voice rose above the crowd.

"Hey, Virginia! There you are! I've been looking all over for you."

Turning on my heel, I found Owen approaching us at a close clip and tried not to let my jaw drop at the sight of him. Tight jeans and an equally tight Fortune Springs Fire Department T-shirt showed off his body to great effect, and his smile did things to my heart that couldn't be entirely healthy, cardiovascularly speaking.

"Owen. Uh, hi—"

Slipping into our small conversation, Owen turned his charming smile on the woman before me, but something shifted in his smile. It was a little less genuine, a little more put-on. I wondered what that meant, but didn't have time to give it a proper examination. "Good to see you, Mrs. Whitlow. How's that old man of yours?"

"Stubborn as always. Wouldn't even come out here with me tonight," she confided.

"That's a shame. He's missing a date with the prettiest woman in the room."

Giggles. Owen seemed to have that effect on people. "Oh, stop it."

At my side, Willa glanced up at me, her eyes questioning. I shrugged, but completed our unspoken conversation just in time for Owen to once again turn the attention of our group back to me.

"Now, what's all this about, Virginia? I thought you were coming to help me with my booth tonight?"

Uh... No. That wasn't ever on the table. We'd never discussed this night or anything of the sort. But I played along, willing with every part of my body for this strange gambit of his to work out.

These uptight school folk were trying every excuse in the book to keep Willa—a perfectly good kid with a bit of a troubled past—from enrolling. They thought just because she had a difficult home life that she couldn't be a good and productive member of their happy little school. They could paper it over with all the phony reasoning they wanted, but I wasn't backing down. And apparently, neither was Owen.

"Well, I was," I said, laying it on maybe a little bit thick, "but we're having a little bit of a problem here."

"And what could that be?"

"It seems that the Helen Hunt Jackson County High School doesn't accept late-year transfers, and so they're telling me Willa here can't get into school until the fall."

Owen's face fell into a confused scowl. "That can't be."

A smile threatened the muscles in my cheeks, and I forced the sensation away to keep up our pretense. It was... strange. I couldn't remember ever having someone in my corner like this before, someone willing to help me navigate a crowd of strangers, just to help.

"But it's true. That's what they're telling me, anyway," I said, letting my shoulders sag slightly.

Owen waved his hand across the aisle, towards a man in a nice suit talking to a gaggle of parents. He had small glasses and kind, tired eyes, the eyes of a man constantly caught in the middle of small-town politics.

"Hey, Principal Hernandez, did you hear this?"

In one easy motion, the principal left his previous conversation and swept into ours. "Hear what, Chief Harris?"

"Virginia here is telling me that you all aren't accepting her friend Willa here until the fall. But that can't be right, can it?"

That question wasn't directed at the principal, but at me. I returned the volley to him in kind. "No, it definitely can't be right, because that's a violation of state and federal law. That's why I came down here, because I knew they wouldn't do something like that. Not to a child who belongs in school."

"So, there must be some mistake, right, sir?" Owen asked.

Only *then* did Owen fix the principal with a heavy stare, one that left no room for misinterpretation. There was a dark tenor to the expression, one I didn't quite understand. Principal Hernandez looked left, then right, at the growing crowd all around us, and flashed Willa a slightly strained smile.

"Why don't you come in on Monday with your grandmother, Miss Holtzman? And we'll get you all sorted out with your class schedule?"

The thrill of victory filled my body. We'd done it. We'd *done it.* Shoving my hand out for a shake, I flashed the biggest grin I was capable of producing. "Thank you so much, sir. It's been a pleasure."

"Yes. And, uh, likewise, I'm sure." That strained smile didn't leave his face as we shook hands. Almost immediately, he turned back to Willa. "Why don't you, uh, take a look around the festival? Maybe have a look at your future career options, hm?"

Almost immediately, he and Mrs. Whitlow practically galloped away, reaching for the first nearby people they could grab in order to avoid any further conversation with us. Not that I particularly cared. All that mattered was Willa, and the bright smile currently dominating her face.

It was the first real smile I'd ever seen from her. Holding out my hands for a low five, I hissed triumphantly, "You're in."

Her hands slapped my own. "I'm in!"

"Wanna have a look around?"

She nodded so hard and so fast, I worried she might give herself whiplash. "Yes, please."

"Meet me back here in fifteen, okay? I promised Calla we'd be home for dinner and she doesn't exactly know we're here."

"Got it."

Almost as quickly as the principal and his secretary had left, Willa disappeared into the crowd, still clutching her books to her chest with one hand, leaving me completely alone in a crowd with Owen Harris.

The man who'd helped make it all possible.

"Well," I said, fully intending to add something to that word, but coming up short almost immediately.

"Well," he echoed.

The air between us was almost awkward and almost comfortable. We danced on the edge of something, and I didn't know if I wanted to fall.

What I did know? Owen Harris would catch me if I did.

"That was…" I cleared my throat when my voice failed me. "Thank you. It means a lot to her. And to me."

"They really weren't going to let her into the school?"

Maybe Owen Harris was the decent guy everyone seemed to think he was, but I still wasn't going to give out the private details of Willa's life to anyone without her permission. I shrugged. "It's complicated. But thank you, for helping me un-complicate it."

"Hey, there are some kids over at my booth. Come with me? I've got candy."

"I was always told never to follow strange men who offer me candy," I said, despite the fact that I was already following him through the crowded aisles of the career fair.

"Oh, I'm strange, am I?"

"Strange as they come, I think. How are the puppies?"

He shoved his hands deep into his pockets, and the dimples deepened in his cheeks. "Cuter by the minute. Do you want to swing by and have a visit? Might help you make your decision about what we discussed yesterday."

"Owen—"

"Don't worry. I'm not trying to rush you. Take all the time you need. I can handle a full Fire House and seven dogs on my own. No problem."

The laughter in his tone coaxed some out from me, too. I raised a questioning eyebrow. "A master multitasker?"

"No, I'll just make my buddies take care of all the Fire House stuff so I can play with the pups all day. That's what we in the management business call *delegating*." We reached the table for the Fortune Springs Fire Department, and he dug into a jar of candy and withdrew a bright red lollipop for me, the kind with the chocolate chewing candy inside. "Here. For you."

There wasn't any way he could know that these were my favorites, right? That I'd already eaten every single one of them in the Bride House. I twirled the candy in my grip, trying to ignore the deep, unsettling questions currently wracking my brain. Impossible. "Thanks. Hey... can I ask you something?"

"Sure."

"Why are you being so nice to me?"

After all, we hadn't started on the right foot. I could practically *feel* his dislike rolling off of him the first time we met. And now... he was doing things like helping me get a sad kid into school and handing me candy and smiling at me like he was made to do it.

A shadow crossed his face. Something like... like shame?

"You told me you thought I didn't like you. I wanted to make sure you knew that wasn't the case."

Suddenly, the air in the gym felt too hot and too close, and with the way he was looking at me, as though I were the only person in the world, I had to wonder if suddenly everyone else had disappeared, leaving us completely alone. But just at that moment, an overeager kid racing down the aisle bumped into me, dropping me squarely back into reality. The kid went straight for Owen's booth, giving me the perfect out. With a small smile and a wave of thanks, I left Owen behind, my mind awhirl.

At that moment, I fully intended to track Willa down and race back to the Bride House, so we could be home in time for the promised dinner with Calla. If there was one thing Calla couldn't stand, it was people who showed up late for dinner, after all.

But a booth about five tables down from Owen's brought my feet to a sudden halt. Centennial State College, with its blue, white, and red table, filled my vision, drawing me towards it.

According to the trifold poster plopped on the table, it was located here, in Fortune Springs, an outlet of a larger community of colleges. A stack of brochures called my name, their siren song luring me closer and closer to the booth.

Yesterday, Owen had mentioned this. Transferring my credits—my master's in psychology with a focus on animal-assisted therapy—writing my dissertation, and riding around Fortune Springs with a van full of puppies, ready to help counsel people and help them feel even a little bit better about their lives. It seemed impossible. Maybe it was. But I took one of the brochures just in case, tucking it under my arm like a shameful secret as I went in search of my pint-sized compatriot.

A few minutes later, we were walking out of the gym when I glanced down at her.

"What are you smiling about down there? That excited for school?"

"Yes." She paused, and her smile only got wider. "And something else."

"What's that?"

"I was right. Chief Harris really does like you."

My stomach twisted. Half hope. Half dread. I hid the feeling behind a smile of my own.

"If you think that, then you *definitely* need to get back into school, little girl."

Chapter Eleven

We *were* late for dinner that night. But all was forgiven once we told Calla the upshot of our evening of escape from the Bride House.

"You got her into school?" she said, nearly dropping the salad bowl in her hands.

"Yeah, we sure did," I said, unable to wipe the glee from my own face. "She starts on Monday. You'll need to go in and get her all signed up, but once I reminded them, very publicly, that it's against the law to deny a child enrollment, they changed their tune pretty quick."

"And Chief Harris helped."

"Willa!"

The little traitor at my side smirked and shrugged as she returned to her overflowing plate of pasta and salad. "What? He did."

I knew that this was going to open up a whole new line of conversation with Calla about the fire chief, but I still couldn't be entirely mad at Willa. Not when she was so excited about everything that had happened tonight. Not when she finally seemed like a kid instead of a small adult who'd had to grow up way too fast for her own good.

Besides, this was what being a kid was all about, right? Getting under the skin of every adult in the vicinity. I figured I could let her have this one, no matter how much of Calla's speculation I'd have to endure now.

"Chief Harris doesn't really do a whole lot of talking out in public," Calla began, her voice slow and deliberate but her eyes sparkling with unspoken mischief. "It must have really drawn a crowd if both of you were involved in this little discussion. No wonder Hernandez folded so quickly."

"I don't think it matters how it happened. All that matters is that Willa's going back to school. Now, we can focus on getting me back to work," I said, hoping to change the subject but knowing that the hope was probably a vain one.

Genuine confusion crossed Calla's face. She reached for her oversized drink tumbler and took a long sip as she sized me up. "Really? You want to go to work?"

"Of course I do."

Lie. One I hoped she wouldn't call me out on.

"That's interesting," she said, putting down her tumbler with a heavy, metallic *thud* on the wooden table beneath. Her voice was breezy and oh-so casual. "Because I saw a college brochure under your arm when you got home. If you wanted to finish up your degree, I'm sure we could work out something part-time for you while you're finishing up school—"

"I don't know if I really want to apply," I said, too quickly, my throat tightening. Stupid. I should have known better than to leave the brochure lying around, but I'd been in such a rush to tell Calla about what had happened down at the high school that I'd forgotten to cover my tracks. I shrugged and twirled a piece of pasta meticulously around my fork, wishing I could twist this talk like I could twist the noodle. "It was just an idea."

"An idea you cooked up with Owen last night? Don't think I've forgotten about your little late-night run up the stairs, missy."

With a flat gaze, I turned to Willa and deadpanned: "Aren't *you* supposed to be the granddaughter here?"

Calla's eyebrows shot up. "As long as you're in this house, young lady, I'll be taking any gossip you've got to give me. Now, spill."

This is going to sound so ridiculous, I thought. But with Calla's eyes on me, I knew I had no choice but to obey and tell her everything. Even if the everything included live animal birth and a high school's career night. When it was all finished, Calla didn't say anything for a long time. She just stared at me, the wrinkles between her eyes deepening as she furrowed her brow. When none of us spoke for a long minute, she finally took her cue.

"So?"

"What do you mean *so*?" I choked, incredulous.

How could she be so nonchalant about this? I mean, I knew she was generally nonchalant about *everything*—it was infuriating, how calm and gritty she was—but still. The way she blinked at me as though I'd told her something exceedingly ordinary was nearly infuriating.

She went back to her pasta, speaking to me between bites and gesturing to me with her fork when it wasn't actively in use.

"I mean what are you going to do about it? You've got the opportunity to do something great—to get your education and start the business you've always wanted. And you're, what? Sitting here, eating my dinner and wringing your hands about whether or not it's the right thing to do?"

Tightness constricted my airways. I glanced over to Willa, who hadn't stopped watching us the entire meal. I wondered if this was what it was like to have siblings. To not only worry about what your parent thought of you, but how your younger sibling saw you, too.

Not wanting to drag even more of my life story in front of Willa—I didn't know if she needed to hear anything about my past right now, not in her state—I went back to my dinner, trying to force down bites of my own even though each one now tasted like sawdust.

"Maybe we shouldn't talk about this right now."

"Anything you have to say about this in front of me, you can surely say in front of Willa. We're all sharing a moment here. Anything you're going through, we can both just as easily learn from."

Not for the first time, I looked at Calla and really examined her. From the way she carried herself about town, not to mention all of the gossip she had at her fingertips, she seemed like the ultimate grand dame of Fortune Springs. A community leader who knew everyone, understood everything, and waited on absolutely no one. But there were moments—like now—when an undercurrent of grief disturbed her smooth waters. It warned that all was not easy and calm in this woman's life. That she'd only become such an important leader in this small town because she'd gained her power and poise through experience.

I wondered if I could ever be like that. If ever, one day, all of the weight I carried could be a shield and a sword instead of a burden. I guessed it wasn't a journey Calla had made alone. And if she hadn't, then I definitely couldn't.

"I just..." How to put this honestly and delicately? I didn't know if it was possible, but I had to try. "Before I came here to Fortune Springs, I was with someone who told me I was stupid. That I wouldn't amount to anything if I wasn't with him. What if he's right? What if I apply and prove that everything he said was exactly true?"

The words came out in a rush—not just of syllables and meaning, but of emotion. I'd never confessed anything so deeply personal out loud. Not to anyone. But when I looked up at Calla to gauge her reaction, she was tossing some more Parmesan on her angel hair pasta, her face unmoved and immovable.

"Oh, I don't think that's what you're worried about. Not at all."

All the air I'd been struggling to keep in my burning lungs came out in a large *whoosh*. Replacing the air proved incredibly difficult. "Excuse me?"

Calla leveled her gaze at me, her stare turning almost unnervingly still. Somehow, it wasn't like she was looking at me anymore. She was looking at my soul. Or my future. Or into my past. Straight into the truth of me. "You're not worried you'll prove him right. You're worried that you'll prove him wrong. And if he's wrong about that, then what *else* has he been wrong about? What other pieces and parts of you have you hidden away because of him? What other bits of yourself will you have to excavate and bring back to life?"

"I—"

The beginning of a sentence came out more from habit than from actually having anything to say. I didn't. No matter how hard I tried to form a coherent reply, nothing came.

From the corner of my eye, I checked in with Willa, who watched us with the riveted enthusiasm of the latest blockbuster's first audience. Everything in me wanted to send her away, but in my heart, I knew Calla was right. From what I understood, Willa's childhood so far hadn't been any kind of picnic. Maybe she had some unlearning of her own to do, too.

"You've already achieved your goal, haven't you?" Calla continued. The stare remained, and I found I couldn't look away once I caught it again. "You escaped. But now, what are you going to do with that freedom? People can still control us even when they're nowhere near us. Are you going to let him do that to you for the rest of your life just because untangling yourself might be hard? Just because it might hurt?"

I wanted to run out of the room. I wanted Calla to wrap her arms around me so I could cry in peace. I wanted to throw plates and burn pictures and wake up tomorrow with no knowledge of the last few years of my life.

I wanted Calla to be wrong. Even though, with every word she spoke, I knew she was right.

My appetite completely gone, I carefully folded my napkin and placed it on the table. Then, my hands replaced it in my lap. It took me longer than I am comfortable admitting, coming up with something to say. Coming up with the strength to speak at all.

"So, what are you saying I should do?"

"Take a vacation to Bali. Learn to trick-ride on a show pony. Start a charity. Have a torrid affair with some handsome man here in town. Take up bread making. That's what *I* would do." She carefully placed a purposeful pause in the middle of her thought. Then, she carefully placed a purposeful hand atop mine. Reassuring. Her hard eyes melted. "But it's not my life and it's not my freedom and I don't get a say in what you do with it. Only *you* can decide what your life is going to look like. And who you're going to let shape it."

The cool air from the vents in the floor did nothing to cool the heat puddling beneath my skin. For the second time tonight, I wanted nothing more than to escape. Only this time, it wasn't a person or a feeling I wanted to escape. It was reality itself. A knowledge I didn't want to obtain but couldn't deny.

I glanced at the waiting stack of cookies in the center of the table, the ones I'd been eyeing since the moment Willa and I walked through the door. Not much of an escape plan, but it was all I had for the moment.

"Do you mind if I take my dessert outside? I think I might need some fresh air, if that's okay."

"Absolutely. Let me walk you."

Not exactly what I'd been asking for, but I should have known that Calla wouldn't let me go that easily. She never did. Together, we walked in silence to the front door of the house, where she stopped and took me in, her hand on the door making it clear I wasn't supposed to leave until she'd gotten the last word.

"I hope you don't think I'm being too hard on you, kiddo."

I took a moment before I answered her with a sigh. "No, I think maybe I need some tough love right about now."

That was the truth, wasn't it? Nothing she'd said—not about me, not about my life here, not about my old life either, had been wrong. And she'd put into words a feeling that had been growing, quiet and prowling, for days now.

Turns out, you can't escape the truth. No matter how much you might try. The truth doesn't fit in a box under your bed. It can't be politely ignored as you pass it down the street. The truth will always find a way to you in the same way the wind seems to do.

"It's just that I really…" A half-dozen emotions flitted across Calla's face, but she schooled them into one of her practiced, frontier tough expressions. She wasn't one to show much depth of feeling, but moments like this reminded me that she couldn't escape from the truth, either. She was starting to care for me, just like I was starting to care for her and Willa. "You've really become a fixture in this old house and Willa looks up to you a lot. I don't think you came to the Bride House by accident. I think you came here for a reason, and I have to believe that reason is to make you better than when you first walked through the door, you know?"

"Yeah. Believe me. I know."

With that, she took her hand off the door, and I went for it. But her words awakened something in me, and now, my mind was a whirl of possibility and… frightening as it was, hope.

"Calla, can I ask you a question before you go?"

"Shoot."

"How do you feel about dogs in the Bride House? Like, six of them?"

Chapter Twelve

It wasn't going to be easy, learning to completely rewrite my life. Calla was right. For so long, escape had been my only real goal. Now, with that out of the way and the rest of my existence sprawled out before me, I had to figure out what I was going to do next.

There was always my first goal. Get out of Fortune Springs, drive to California, start a new life all by myself on some remote beach where no one could ever find me again. On many levels, that was appealing to me still. Waking up to the golden sunshine every morning. Falling asleep to the gentle, soothing rush of the moon pushing and pulling the tides against the rocky sands. Having an existence that was entirely mine.

But then, there was a voice in the back of my head—one that sounded exactly like Calla—that questioned *why* that was the future I'd concocted for myself. Why had I envisioned a future where I barely had any other contact with anyone? Where I isolated myself on the edge of the world and spent the rest of my days with nothing but the sun and the ocean?

Was... was she right? Was I too afraid? Afraid of people? Of letting myself get close to them?

I wasn't sure. The only thing I *was* sure of was that, if it was true, I wasn't going to keep letting it control me. And that's how I found myself marching down the street, slice of pie from Calla's dinner still in my hand, towards the Engine House. Towards Owen.

"Hello? Owen?"

Right. Of course. Maybe he was asleep. Or maybe he was out. Out on a date, maybe. A twinge of something unfamiliar shot through me at that thought. I knocked again.

"Owen?"

"Yeah, sorry," a familiar voice called from inside the walls. "Come on in."

I hesitated, not wanting to just let myself into a near-stranger's house. But once I remembered that I'd done exactly that the last time I'd been in this house, I turned the handle without another minute's thought.

Entering now, not in a rush to help a dog give birth, I allowed myself to take a closer look at the place. Like the Bride House, it had a touch of Victorian charm, but unlike the Bride House, it had an ultra-modern half of the house in which the fire engines were kept. Inside, I could only see the doors leading to that part, but in here, on the first floor, I could see the walls decorated with pictures of the firemen's classes past, news clippings about their good deeds, and a lack of feminine touch that reminded me why the Bride House and its Settlement Initiative had been invented in the first place.

Listening to the sounds of the house, I tried to feel my way towards Owen—not in the oversized dining room, nor in the tiny kitchen. Turning towards the living room, I marched there.

Only to find him sprawled on a couch, half-asleep and covered in small puppies presumably using his body heat for warmth. Not just any part of his body heat, though. The body heat radiated by his bare chest.

I'm sure the world didn't *literally* stop at the sight of a chisel-jawed, sharp-eyed man cradling a litter of puppies against his incredibly sexy stomach, but that's how it felt. As if the world paused for the briefest of moments to let me behold him, before rushing into double-time to catch up.

Jolting up at the sight of me, he was just awake enough to stop himself short and keep himself from totally disturbing the puppies.

"I'm—"

"Oh my God, I'm so sorry."

In an attempt to avert my gaze from him, I searched for anywhere else to put my eyes. A glimpse in one of the room's mirrors rewarded me with the treat of my own reflection, which was currently tinted allergic-reaction red. But when he spoke again, his voice was confused.

"Sorry about what? I asked you to come in here."

"I didn't realize you were, uh—the puppies covered your—"

Please don't make me say it. Please don't make me talk about your perfect body. I am begging.

His face blanched as he realized without my having to spell it out. "Oh. Right. Give me a second. I'm sorry about that."

"No, really, it was my fault. Here."

My eyes landing on an old, ratty sweatshirt that must once have been black but had since faded to a deep gray, I picked it up and blindly tossed it in his direction, still not wanting to look too closely at him.

"You really *are* skittish around men, aren't you?"

If I was really so skittish, or if I was as skittish as I was a week ago, I wouldn't be in this house alone with you right now, I wanted to say, but I didn't, because I could hear that same teasing tone in his voice, and knew he was trying to lighten the mood, a fact for which I was supremely grateful.

"What's that supposed to mean?" I asked, trying to match his tone and failing miserably. Hard to do when I was still more than a little breathless.

"It's just… Not to brag or anything…"

Too late, I thought to myself with an internal smirk that I couldn't match on the outside.

"But most women wouldn't run away at the sight of these chiseled abs."

That was the problem, though. I didn't *want* to run away from the chiseled abs. I wanted to run my hands across them and kiss them and see how the rest of him looked when in a similar state of undress. That strange feeling of want, that unfamiliar sensation of desire, was what freaked me out in that moment, not anything to do with Owen and his abs themselves.

Placing myself on the couch, I began giving most of my attention to the pups he'd left behind. Ignoring my feelings was easier when I had six tiny animals fighting for scritches. "You know," I said, mirroring his teasing tone. "Saying 'not to brag' immediately before bragging doesn't change the fact that you're bragging, right?"

"Listen, I just wanted you to know, if we're going to be doing this together for awhile—" He stopped himself short, and I didn't dare look up from the puppies to investigate his expression. "I mean, if you're going to be in town for awhile, I just want you to know that you're safe with me. No need to be skittish."

"If I'm safe with you, I'm sure you'll prove it."

"I—"

Before he could protest again and assure me that no, I really *could* trust him, I shot him a silencing look. In most other situations, I wouldn't have dared to be so forward. So aggressive. But after my talk with Calla... I figured it was time to take some risks. Time to see how much the bonds to my old life would give and stretch. "I think a lot of people talk a big game. But in my experience, the old saying is true. Actions speak much, much louder than words."

He wasn't looking at me straight on now, but from under a dark, thick curtain of lashes that betrayed his uncertainty. How strange to see such a powerful man with such a position of leadership in his community seem... almost insecure. "Well, how am I doing so far?"

It didn't take much consideration to answer that. "Better than anyone else. This is the longest I've been alone with a man in a long time." This wasn't exactly true, but for our purposes in this moment, it was. "Besides... if you're willing, then I think you're going to have a lot *more* time to prove that you're trustworthy."

"Oh, yeah?"

"Calla won't let me take the puppies. She says the house is a town landmark, and because it needs to be kept in perfect condition, I can't take the puppies with me any time soon."

"Oh."

Was that a note of disappointment I heard in that one breath of a word? Or was I just projecting my own wishful thinking onto him?

"But… She set up a fund for me, as part of the Settlement Initiative, so I can pay for their food and care and… I was thinking about the possibility of a partnership." When he didn't immediately answer, my stomach dropped. "How does that sound?"

"What, exactly, would something like that entail?"

Follow-up questions weren't exactly ecstatic agreement, but I tried not to let myself break at the thought. "I'll look after the dogs. You wouldn't really need to do much of anything. You'll just need to, you know, put a roof over their heads. I'll take care of the walks and the training and the feeding and all of that, and you just keep them, you know?"

A small stampede of rolly puppy bodies made their way into my lap. Soft snoots and tiny, wrinkled legs tumbled onto me, but still, I tried to keep my eye on the prize here. "And if we do this, if we go into a partnership together, we're going to have to spend a lot of time together. Is that alright?"

He didn't say anything for a moment. I scrambled to speak again. Worry gripped the back of my neck. A moment ago, things had seemed right between us, but now, I couldn't tell if I was winning or losing this battle. The rambling began.

"Because if it isn't alright, then I can figure out some other way to sort all of this out. Maybe there's a kennel or something in a nearby town, or maybe I could—"

"Virginia."

"What?"

Something about the way he said my name… it was almost like hearing it for the first time. I didn't know how to feel about that, or the shameful, twin realization that I never wanted him to stop saying it.

This time, when I braved a look at his face, his mood was perfectly legible. He wasn't hiding from me. His smile told me he'd been messing with me, trying to draw me out, and I'd fallen prey to his trap. Apparently, that was one of his favorite hobbies.

"Do you really think I wouldn't want to spend more time with you?"

"Well, you're busy, and I'm sure you have a lot going on, and—"

His smile only widened. "The puppies can stay here. After all, they *are* my dog's fault."

"Don't say that," I cooed, pressing my hand to the mother's ears as if I was going to cover them up and keep her from hearing the slander. "They're your dog's sweet, baby angels. You should say that instead."

"I'm not going to say that." He chuckled. "But they can definitely stay. And so can you."

"Thanks." And I meant it, with all of my heart. "It'll be nice not to be so alone."

I hadn't meant to say something so pathetic-sounding, and I regretted the words as soon as they were out of my mouth. Owen took it in his stride, though, bending down beside the couch to get a little puppy attention for himself.

"Right. You have me. And Polka. And puppies one to six, whatever we're going to name them. And you have Calla and Willa."

"How strange," I muttered.

"What's so strange about that?"

What was it about this man that sent my mouth off without my permission? Clearing my throat, I tried to explain it as best I could without making myself seem even worse than I already appeared.

"I just thought... When I started over here in Fortune Springs, I thought I'd be going it on my own from now on. That I'd be this totally independent shadow, isolated and remote. That no one could touch me."

"But...?"

A small smile pressed at my lips. "I mean, I definitely didn't plan on accidentally walking in on a Dalmatian in need of a midwife. Or her light-headed owner who was going to pass out at the first sight of blood. But Fortune Springs is getting to me. And so are the people and puppies who live there."

"I wasn't going to pass out. I was going to throw up. There's a big difference there."

The laughter—his and my own—tickled the center of my chest. Part of me hated how such simple things, like laughing with another person or being alone with a man, seemed like absolute revelations. I hated that I'd wasted so much time feeling so miserable and calling it love. But Calla was right. If I didn't face these feelings, fight them, and move past them, then I was never *really* going to be free at all, was I?

"You're really not so bad, you know," I said, letting the tail end of my laughter carry the words.

"Well, thank you," he replied, putting a teasingly modest hand over his heart. "I try not to be."

"You seemed so scary at first. Everyone said you had a secret, soft underbelly—"

"They did?"

"Mm-hm. But I didn't believe them. I guess they were right after all."

"What changed your mind?"

"Besides the way you're cradling those puppies right now?"

For the first time, he looked down and properly took in the picture of himself—a handsome, gentle man cradling small animals like he was made to do it. "Ah. Good point."

In reality, there was about a half-dozen other reasons, at least, that I'd started to believe everyone about him. It wasn't just the puppies or the way he looked after this Fire House. It was Calla's unfailing trust in him. It was the way he'd intervened between me and the high school principal so I could get Willa into school. It was the way he'd offered to sit on the porch and eat brownies with me so I wouldn't have to go inside a stranger's house if I didn't want to.

It was the way he looked after his dog during her birth and the way he told me he didn't want me believing he didn't like me.

It was his smile and the tenderness of his touch.

"Did they really say that about me?" he asked, after a companionable quiet, intercut only by the loudness of my thoughts and the whining of one of the puppies. "That I'm secretly soft?"

"Calla did. She said you weren't nearly as scary as you tried to make everyone believe. Turns out, she was right. At least, I think she was."

"Well, we all know how much she loves to be right about everything."

"So, you're going to be okay? Co-parenting these puppies with me?"

The smile he flashed me then could have lit up an entire city block. That's how powerful it was. How electric it made me feel. "It *will* ruin my apparently rock-solid reputation as the town's scariest loner, but yeah, I think I can help you look after them."

Chapter Thirteen

After my suggestions of naming the puppies after various horror movie villains or Denver Broncos were rejected, and after I'd vetoed Owen's idea of naming them for the tribes of *Battlestar Galactica*—Sagittaron was a *terrible* name for a puppy, in my opinion—we decided on naming them after the peaks of the Rocky Mountains. Borah, Wheeler, Pike, Bianca, Wilson, and Antora.

Okay, so not *much* better than Sagittaron, but still. Over the next few days, the puppies took to their new names and our co-parenting well.

The men of the Fire House, on the other hand? Well, they were all nice enough. All polite. All remembered their manners around a lady. But I found it hard to be in a house with so many men at once, even when Owen was nearby, so I didn't spend much time inside with them. As soon as the puppies' eyes opened, I acquired a set of six tiny vests and a connector leash so I could take them on as many long walks as their little legs would allow them.

That was the day I became the most popular woman in Fortune Springs. Apparently, facing down the school principal and taking up with the loner fire chief and being a stranger from out of town was alright as long as you did it while walking around town with six adorable puppies.

As the days passed, I tried my shameful best to keep my emotional distance from Owen, a feat that proved impossible considering my daily walks both started and ended at his Fire House. And considering that he found me every time I so much as approached the front door, even trying felt foolish.

But it was one thing to dive headfirst into raising puppies and starting a college application. It was another thing entirely to give in to the strange feelings Owen Harris gave me.

For a few days, I even asked Willa and Calla to take the puppies on a walk, just so I could get some space and clear my head. After all, there were other things that made avoiding him difficult. Like that time I found him washing the fire engine in nothing but a surprisingly short pair of shorts and a soaking wet T-shirt that clung to his abs like hard, rippling bark on a tree. Or that time I dreamed about him wearing absolutely nothing, leaving me breathless when I woke up.

Or this morning, when I answered a knock on the front door of the Bride House to find him standing there in all his backlit glory, holding two cups of coffee in those strong, dream-inducing hands of his.

I blinked, hard and fast, and wondered for a moment if this was another dream. I knew better than to ask, obviously, because if he did turn out to be real, then I would basically be confessing that I'd been dreaming of him, which I didn't *ever* want to admit. When his image didn't vanish, though, I dropped my jaw to speak, only for no sound to come out.

Thankfully, Owen picked up the conversational baton with one of those lazy, friendly, *you're the only person in the world* smiles of his. The kind of smile that made the back of my neck heat up with forbidden excitement. How did he manage that? It all seemed so effortless for him.

"Good morning."

There was only one reason I could imagine for him coming here instead of meeting me at the Engine House. My heartbeat picked up a pace. "Is something wrong. Are the dogs—"

"No, they're fine. They're actually all still sleeping off a play date with some of the guys who came over yesterday. Ran them ragged. I just thought…" It was his turn to lose his words. After a second of silence, he thrust the cup in his left hand out to me. "Here."

Despite the familiar golden sleeve on the cup—which belonged to Coffeebou, a small shop in town that boasted a sunglass-wearing caribou drinking coffee as its logo—I stared at it as though I'd never seen the like before in my life.

"What's this?"

"Coffee."

The warmth of the drink radiated through the heat-resistant sleeve, and though I'd been careful to take it without so much as brushing against Owen's skin, my entire body came alive with the warmth of the drink.

"Oh."

What the hell else was I supposed to say? The action—buying someone a cup of coffee and bringing it to them—was so simple and sweet. And yet, I couldn't remember the last time someone had done it for me. I didn't have the words for how it made me feel.

Honestly, I didn't even *know* how it made me feel. I couldn't read my own emotions, much less string them into a coherent *thank you*.

That was the thing about moving here, to Fortune Springs, that I hadn't entirely expected. All my life, I'd pretty much been on my own. Sure, I'd had family around, and shortly after I'd left home, I'd found my first, big, spectacularly awful relationship. The "before" time of my life, though, I'd mostly had to fend for myself. I was surrounded by people, obviously, but still, I often found myself alone. Scrounging what I could from the kitchen to make my own dinners when I was a kid. Counting the hours until my partner came back when I was in a relationship.

I wasn't used to people caring about me. Or thinking about me. A coffee might have been a simple thing, a *nothing* for everyone else, but to me, it was more shocking than a kick to the stomach and more touching than… well, anything I'd experienced in a long, long time.

These sorts of moments happened more in Fortune Springs than I cared to admit. Whether it was Calla offering me a cup of tea and a heaping plate of cookies in the afternoon or Willa asking me for help with a personal essay for her language arts class or the fact that the coffee shop owner always remembered my name and order, I felt part of something here.

As I turned these thoughts over in my head, I'd almost forgotten about Owen's presence entirely. My quiet prompted him to mutter, almost sheepishly:

"It's for you."

"Right. Yeah. Obviously. Um, let me go upstairs and grab my wallet—"

"Why? Are you going somewhere?"

"Well, you brought me coffee—"

"Yeah. As a gift."

My chest tightened. Oh, no. It was even worse than I'd feared. He hadn't just brought me a coffee for convenience's sake. He'd bought it to be nice.

"A gift," I repeated, the word and concept suddenly foreign and untranslatable on my tongue.

When was the last time I'd gotten a gift? A real one, with no strings attached?

"Yeah, you always come over with a cup of coffee and I thought, you know, maybe this morning you'd like to take a walk with me. And have some coffee."

Shifting on my feet, I mentally ran through my current dilemma over and over again. The last thing I wanted was to seem ungrateful or to offend the man currently looking after my puppies. The man I was starting to like quite a great deal, in spite of my better judgment. But, still, my alarm bells blared and all the red flags unfurled. My suspicions were out in full force. Not because of anything he'd done, of course. But because that's just who I was. A suspicious person who'd been trained into that way of thinking over too much time and too many mistakes.

"That's really sweet," I finally said, looking at the coffee cup instead of him. The scents of cinnamon and vanilla and dark roast—my usual order—filled my nose, almost making me light-headed. "Thoughtful."

"Are you sure? You look like you're about to be sick. Did I get the wrong thing? Are you—"

"What's the catch?"

This time, he was the one who repeated a word as though he'd never heard it before.

"The catch?"

"Come on. People don't do stuff like this without there being a catch. What's the coffee in exchange for? What do you want from me?"

That was how it had worked my entire life. My mother gave me attention only when she needed me to do something. The man I'd left behind in George would give me dresses a size too small so I would lose weight; jewelry so I'd feel like I owed him something for it. Compliments so I'd work all the harder to get them once he started withholding them again. Relationships were transactional. That's how I understood them.

Coffee was never just coffee. At least, not in my experience.

"Nothing. I mean, I was hoping you'd come on that walk with me, but you really don't have to. I mean, I understand if you don't want to."

God, I could almost believe he was sincere when he looked at me like that. Years of disappointment and disaster told me to ignore him, to thank him for the coffee and close the door in his face, but my feet itched to move off of this porch and out onto whatever walk he was contemplating.

Not just my feet. My heart, too.

With all the humor I could muster, I raised one eyebrow and tried to look droll. "Aren't you worried a fire's going to happen while you're gone, Mr. Fire Chief?"

Over the last week, I'd noticed he rarely left the fire station, a fact I could only assume had to do with his devotion to his duty. But he just shrugged and swallowed back a fresh sip of coffee.

"Doc's there monitoring the bell and he's got me on speed-dial," he said, referencing a much older, retired gentleman who worked around the Engine House sometimes. "I'm not too worried. Besides, I think I could use a walk."

"Me too," I said, surprised to find that I meant it.

"Shall we?"

Shall we? It was such an old-fashioned phrase, one I hadn't ever heard outside of black and white movies, but the way he said it sent warm chills down my back. It was both old-fashioned and modern, a real question and a tease.

I knew I needed to resist. To ignore him. To get on with my work and look after the puppies and start outlining my entrance essays for my application and, and, and...

And his smile was too irresistible. Crooked and genuine, he focused it directly on me. I was useless against its powers.

Still, I found it hard to believe that a guy like this—infuriating and mystifying as he might have been at times—wanted to spend any kind of time with me. Sure, we had the puppies together, but that I could write off as necessity rather than want. This... this was something different, and I had a hard time accepting it.

"Are you sure you want me to come? You don't have to—"

"I want to. If *you* want to, of course. I mean, I was just thinking about how you haven't been out much in town, have you?"

"No," I said, my lips tugging into a wry smile as I wordlessly reminded him of school and puppies and everything *else* I'd been dealing with. "I've been kind of busy, actually."

"Right, and that's a real shame. Remember when you said this town didn't have any culture? I was thinking maybe today we could take a stroll around. Give you the real Fortune Springs Cultural Tour. If you're up for it, that is."

"I am. I'd really like that."

"You would?"

"Don't sound so surprised," I said, trying to play off the fact that I, myself, was surprised. "You're pretty charming when you want to be."

"I don't think anyone in this town has *ever* called me charming."

"What? Are *brooding, solitary* and *frowny* more common?"

He chuckled, the warm sound filling me up from the inside out and drawing out my own smile. "You forgot stoic and anti-social, but yeah. Those are definitely more common than charming."

I shook my head. "They don't know what they're missing."

If I'd known that meeting his gaze then would have filled my heart with fireworks, I absolutely wouldn't have done it. I would have stared at my boots and tried to pretend he didn't exist. As it was, though, I *did* meet his gaze, and found it particularly hard to pull away once I'd begun.

Eventually, mercifully, he cleared his throat and motioned towards the Bride House gate.

"We should probably get started. Come on. I have so many places I want to show you."

"Lead the way."

Chapter Fourteen

He hadn't been kidding when he'd talked about the expansive history and culture of the town. At first, I wrote off his enthusiasm as a thinly veiled joke, but truth be told, the longer we walked around, the more I fell in love with this place. He pointed out small architectural details of Fortune Springs—the eagles carved into the corbels of the library, the bronze statue of a squirrel offering an acorn to a hungry bear—and welcomed me into its history with his stories. All of that, I loved. But it wasn't just the tour that made me come alive.

Everywhere we went, someone knew our names. People waved on the street, smiled and asked about our day. It was strange, feeling like I belonged somewhere. Strange. Forbidden. But nice, too.

The tour continued when we reached the center of town, with its timber-framed buildings and its view of the expansive mountain range out at the far end of town. Owen put on his best historical documentary voice as I wandered around. Everywhere he led me, I'd been before, but I'd never taken the time to really drink in and absorb any of it before.

"So, the town was founded originally in 1871, when gold-panners and trappers started to move into the valley here. But the problem was that the *real* gold wasn't in the water up in those mountains. It was the trees. So, pretty soon, when they realized that, the entire place converted into a logging town."

"Yeah, I've heard plenty about the logging operation," I said, mentally shuddering at the reminder of a long, long conversation I'd had with a stranger outside of the Post Office a few days ago, a kindly man, but one who wouldn't stop talking about timber. "It's, uh…"

How to put this in a way that wouldn't insult him? I didn't know how. Thankfully, he didn't make me even attempt. He finished the prompt for me.

"Painfully boring?"

"Yes." I practically sighed from the relief of it. A laugh pulsed at the tip of my tongue. "I got cornered for about ten straight minutes of wood talk outside of the Post Office. And I don't mean that in the fun way."

The words just came out before I could stop them. Immediately, I opened my mouth to retract them, to take them back and pretend they'd never happened, but I should have known Owen would be too sharp for that. Drawing his face up into a scandalized expression, he pressed a hand to his heart.

"What fun way would that be, Miss Virginia? Did you just make a double entendre?"

Oh, God, did I just *giggle*? I struggled to pull myself back together and school my expression into something more appropriate.

"I'm sure I don't know what you mean."

"Well, if all of the logging talk bores you to tears, let me tell you about a little town secret. Come on."

Without any fanfare, he took my hand in his as though it was the most natural thing in the world. I flinched at first, surprised by the contact, but relaxed into it when I realized how perfectly our hands fit together. How gentle and easy his grip was. He wasn't holding me to keep me, but to let *me* keep *him*.

"So, this is—"

"The Town Hall," I finished, looking up at the familiar building. I hadn't gotten much of a tour when I'd first moved here, but the giant, brass letters hammered into the facade spelling out TOWN HALL pretty much gave the place away.

"Wasn't always, though. See those names up there? Inscribed over the clock?"

"Mm-hm."

Stepping forward, I narrowed my eyes up towards the clock at the center of the building. *Marylou Kelly. Li Na Liu. Edna Gunnel. Sonia Caraveo.*

"Those are the names of our town's original signatory founders. And the first town council. Our first mayor was the madame of the establishment where they worked."

"I beg your pardon?"

I stared up at the names surrounding the clock as Owen continued his historical explainer.

"They wanted a good town to live in, just like everyone else did. They figured if they were in charge, they'd be in the best position to make that happen. They were even the ones who organized the funds to build the Bride House, which they used whenever men ordered brides from back east. Now, it's being used for a pretty similar purpose, I guess."

So *that's* why they called it the Bride House. Sure, I'd seen the photographs in the house of the house filled with women, but I hadn't quite guessed what all of them meant. Now, I knew.

"That's incredible."

"Strong women here in Fortune Springs. That much hasn't changed in almost a hundred and fifty years, at least."

"I hope you're not lumping me into that category."

"Why wouldn't I?"

He asked it so innocently. As if he really believed I *was* strong. If only I could believe it myself. Rolling my eyes, I nudged him with my shoulder.

"I thought you were giving me a tour, not psychoanalyzing me."

"Can't I do both?"

"Keep walking, Doctor Freud."

We'd been out for hours now. The skies above us had changed, and all of my body ached with all of the walking and the sightseeing. Not to mention my brain, which felt like it was about to explode from all of the new information.

Or possibly from the pressure systems moving above us. The weather forecasts assured us it wasn't going to rain today, but the clouds threatened overhead as we marched through the dense forest to the east of town.

He promised me a tromp through the woods would be worth it. I had to believe him. But right about now, all I wanted was a shower and a cup of hot chocolate and a long nap on my favorite couch in the living room of the Bride House.

"So," I said, slightly breathless from the trekking. "We've seen Panner's Peak, every inch of town, and tried three of your favorite food spots, including that old lady's house where you just asked her if she had any leftover pie."

"Mrs. Hibbert loves making pies. The odds that she had some leftovers in her house that she was looking to get rid of were pretty good!"

Despite the ache in my lungs and my legs, I couldn't help but laugh. The old woman *had* leftover pie, and she'd offered it over happily. Blueberry. My favorite.

Traveling around Fortune Springs wasn't much different from traveling on my own, but in having Owen by my side, pointing out all of the town's small details that I might have missed, I felt like I saw it now with new eyes. Not only because of all the things Owen taught me, but because I realized there were so many little things I hadn't allowed myself to notice before.

Like the way everyone knew my name. And smiled when I walked by. And stopped to ask me how I was liking things around town.

People here cared about me. Even people I didn't know. What a strange, delightful, utterly confusing thing to discover.

The woods around us towered, stretching up towards the sky and creating our own personal walking cocoon. The wind brought whispers of fresh pine and the scent of stone straight to my nose, and I breathed the air in deeper and deeper with every step we took into the density of the forest.

"And now that my stomach is full and my legs are tired, where the hell are we?" I asked, pressing onward through the brush at his side.

"If you'll just step this way, I think you'll agree that the walk was worth it."

"At least it is pretty shady and breezy. It may not have saved my muscles, but I'm glad I'm not sweating."

"I once heard Calla say that ladies don't sweat; they shimmer," Owen said, striding forward with a chuckle.

I tried not to dwell on how easy the conversation was between us now. How casually we navigated from one topic to the next. How much he managed to make me laugh.

"Speaking of Calla... What's the deal there? Sometimes you two seem like you're on the same page and sometimes..."

"We don't see eye to eye on a lot of things. Like the Bride House. But... I guess she's got her heart in the right place."

My heart felt like it was about to fly away with the next strong breeze. Was I... Did I... had *I* been the reason he'd changed his mind about the Bride House?

No, of course not. That was silly, wishful thinking.

Wasn't it?

"You should give her another chance," I nudged. "She's... She's not at all what I expected and definitely what I needed, you know?"

He was ahead of me now, blocking the space between the two trees ahead. He leveled his attention at me, and sized me up for a long moment. From anyone else, the stare might have been unnerving. It might have made me want to turn and run as far away as I could get, as fast as I could go. But there wasn't a hint of possessiveness or coldness in him. He looked at me like he couldn't wait to understand me. To know me even better than he did now.

"No, I don't know. I've got to say: you're still a complete mystery to me."

The fluttering in my heart kicked into overdrive, and I marched forward, trying to deflect my feelings as best I could. "There's not much to know. I like horror movies and snacking and my favorite chore is scrubbing the floors in the kitchen at the Bride House. I love puppies and sunsets and *short* walks. My favorite color is green. My favorite book is *Rebecca*. If I were any animal, I think I'd be a—"

That's when I shouldered past him, and realized that we weren't in the forest anymore. We were somewhere I'd never been before. A clearing. No, not a clearing. Here, at the curving base of a mountain in the distance, sat a beautiful, glistening lake surrounded on most sides by trees and fresh flowers. In the distance, I could see a small cabin with a handful of small watercraft waiting. Further beyond that, I noticed a road that must have led back towards town. Everything was painted in greens and blues and bright pastels, like someone had dumped an impressionist painter's palette here and left it.

It… it was the most beautiful place I'd ever been.

"*Wow.*"

"*Wow* is not an animal, you know," Owen snarked at my side.

"How can you joke like that when you're facing this?"

"I can't help it. Teasing you has become, like, second nature to me now."

I shot him a look, hoping to hide the fact that I happened to like it when he teased me. He merely shrugged.

"And I guess I've seen this view about a million times."

"I couldn't ever get tired of a place like this."

"This is Folly's Lake. It freezes over in the winter for skating, but right now, it's kind of perfect, isn't it?"

Perfect didn't even begin to describe it. A mountain lake plopped right here near the town where I lived? It was beyond anything I'd ever imagined, like a scene ripped straight from a fairy tale and tucked away here for me to find.

"I can't believe this has been here this whole time and I hadn't noticed it."

"Well, that's the problem with most people. Myself included. There's so much beauty all around us, but we're so wrapped up in our own things that we…"

His eyes met mine. I didn't realize I'd taken my gaze away from the lake to look at him, but there he was, looming larger than life in my vision and so painfully handsome I almost regretted tearing myself away.

"… that we don't see it. Sometimes not until it's too late."

I allowed us to lapse into silence. For the first time since we'd started this little tour, neither of us spoke or even tried to. Silence in this place was better than a million years of conversation anywhere else, and I was going to absorb it.

At least, that's what I tried to do. Instead, my mind and my heart wouldn't let it go, what he'd just said. It seemed meaningful, that stare we shared when he said most people ignored beauty until it was too late. Surely, he couldn't be talking about me.

Could he?

My mind turned over the possibilities, again and again, until suddenly, something shattered my concentration.

"Is that…" I looked heavenward, where the clouds were moving quickly on the southerly wind, straight above them. "Is that rain?"

Almost immediately, as if someone above had heard me and decided to accept the challenge, the skies began to open up. One drop became five, which became twenty, which became the beginnings of a thunderstorm.

Owen looked at the skies and shook his head with a wry smile. "Well, at least I know there won't be any fires anytime soon."

The crash of thunder interrupted my laughter.

"Oh, no!"

"Come on," Owen said, taking my hand as if it was the most natural thing in the world to do. "Let's get somewhere safe and dry!"

Chapter Fifteen

When I'd decided to try my hand at this new life—really try, not just sleepwalk through it—this wasn't exactly what I'd had in mind. Throwing myself into a potential job? Yes. Raising six puppies with a handsome firefighter? Also, yes. Trying to get back into school? Sure. But getting caught in the rain and having to take shelter in a rickety shack at the edge of a sprawling lake? Being stuck with that handsome firefighter in a cozy place while his wet clothes and hair stuck to him and the chill brought out the pink in his lips? Wanting him to wrap his arms around me and banish that chill from my entire body with his own?

No. No, I definitely hadn't predicted that. Or wanted it.

All around us, the world seemed to conspire to bring us closer. The winds rattled the trees by the lake, creating a cacophony of sound and an impenetrable maze of impassable branches barring our escape. The rain came down in steady, hazy drops that threatened to make us even more wet and miserable than we already were. The lightning caught the roving planes of the lake, flashing warning signs through the windows every few heartbeats.

The storm was here. Which meant if we wanted to be safe, we needed to be here, too.

It wasn't an ideal situation. In fact, I'd go as far to say that it was the *least ideal* situation I could have found myself in the middle of. I didn't do well with storms, which was why I focused all of my energy inside of the house instead of outside it.

"You know, you're pretty good at that," I said, watching Owen carefully tend the room's fireplace. Warmth began to shift the cold, stale air of the place into something more manageable.

"What?"

"Making a fire. I would have thought a fireman would want to destroy fires, not make them."

Owen shook his head, suddenly serious. "Anything can be good as long as it's done safely. Especially fire."

The conversation lapsed then, and Owen's face turned into something like deep thought. Curled up under the slightly worn blanket Owen had given me when we'd walked in here, the sudden lack of distraction meant I had nothing to do but think of the storm outside. I tried to focus on my breathing. On my heartbeat. On the crackles of wood and blaze. But it wasn't working. I was holding the blanket to me with the kind of white-knuckle grip you usually only see in drowning men trying to keep hold of their life preservers.

"Are you okay?" Owen asked, once he'd left the fire.

A clash of thunder rolled outside of the windows and straight through my body. I hated that feeling. Hated feeling weak in front of another person. He'd already seen me like this once before—when he'd been fixing the leak in the Bride House and caught me when the thunder made me flinch—but that didn't stop the humiliation I felt now. I kept my reply as short as I could manage. "I don't really like the rain."

"Yeah, I can see that. Come here. Let's get you closer to the heat."

From my place across the room, I studied him as he opened his arms and waited for me to move. This was another one of those decisions—one that could change everything. I never really trusted people, and certainly not him. This was a moment when I'd have to decide if I trusted him now. So, I decided to only do it halfway. Picking myself up and closing the creaking-floored distance between us, I moved into the crook of his arm.

But my entire body was stiff. I didn't relax into him or accept his comfort easily. But it was a start.

"Is that better?" he asked, his warm breath tickling my ear. This time, my shiver had nothing to do with my wet body or the threatening storm outside.

"I'm not cold. I'm just… with the lightning and the wind and everything—"

He offered his second hand, to pull me in closer. His eyes were hesitant. Tentative. Questioning.

"May I?"

"I'd rather you didn't."

It was an impulse, a knee-jerk reaction, not to him, but to everything else. A man having two hands on me? Not something I usually appreciated. That meant he had control, and there was nothing I wanted less right now than to be out of control of my own body. To my surprise, he didn't push me or pressure me to giving in. Instead, his hand immediately dropped, and the offer dissolved.

Or, was I really surprised at all? Owen Harris had never disrespected me before. Never pushed my boundaries.

I pulled my blanket tighter around me, a defense mechanism against the *everything* of this moment.

"Of course. Do you…" He paused, a weighted pause that I didn't have the key to deciphering. "Do you want to talk about it? Sometimes that makes me feel a hell of a lot better."

He was trying to be nice to me, trying to be good and gentlemanly and friendly and everything kind. But all I wanted was to run away. Between the rain and his sudden closeness, all of the anxieties I'd been trying to move past now heightened all around me.

"Why did you bring me here? Why did you take me out today?"

"Because you're new in town and you seemed like you needed a friend."

"I don't," I said, the edges of my vision darkening and the truth refusing to come from between my tense jaw. "I don't need friends. I don't need anyone."

He gave a dry, almost cold laugh. I watched as he brushed a stray speck of dust from his boots. "That's not true. I know better than anyone that people need people. There isn't a soul on this earth that can survive this life thing without someone else helping them get through it."

Protesting seemed like the right thing to do, but a question bubbled to my lips before I could. "What do you mean, you know that better than anyone?"

"I'm a pretty quiet guy. I don't get out much. It can be a pretty lonely life. A pretty sad one sometimes."

"Maybe *you* needed a friend, then. Not me."

"Maybe you're right."

"But you could have any friend you wanted. You didn't need me."

"No. But I wanted you."

I didn't know how it was possible, but I managed to pull the blanket even tighter around myself. Soon, I'd probably be cutting off my circulation.

"It just doesn't make any sense," I muttered.

"I guess it wouldn't to a person with a big mouth and small self-esteem."

"Was that supposed to be charming?"

"It was supposed to be honest. You don't have a very high opinion of yourself, do you?"

"You wouldn't either, if you were in my position," I muttered.

"See? There you go again."

"What?"

"You say these deeply tragic things like you're giving a weather report or like you're telling someone what kind of coffee you prefer."

"I do not," I protested, peeling away from his light embrace and turning to face him. Now, I wasn't afraid of giving him the full force of my attention.

"Yes, you do. And you tell me things about yourself—tell me that you want to try, that you want to be my friend, and then avoid me even though we're both supposed to be raising those dogs together."

"I don't avoid you."

"Come on. I want to understand you better."

"Yeah, well, we don't always get what we want."

"I like you, Virginia. I know that might seem absolutely impossible to you, but I do. I think you're kind and gentle and quietly funny and so lonely that you wouldn't know real friendship if it bit you on the ear. Part of liking you, part of wanting to be your friend, is wanting to actually *know* you. It was a simple question to begin with. Why don't you like the rain?"

I stared at him but couldn't find my voice to answer his question.

"It's nothing, really."

"I'm not going to go anywhere. The truth isn't going to make me hightail it in the other direction."

"I know," I said, muttering the words against the legs of my jeans. "That's the problem."

"Me wanting to stay is the problem?"

"Yes. Because I didn't come here to Fortune Springs because I wanted to make friends or put down roots or stay. But because I want, one day, to leave."

Chapter Sixteen

I had to believe that, at the beginning of the day, Owen hadn't started with the intention of cornering me in a shack and getting me to divulge all of my secrets. That he hadn't brought me out here to the middle of nowhere, on a day that predicted rain, just so he could needle me into confessing the hidden truths of my past.

I had to believe that because I still wanted to like him. But even if I didn't, I couldn't be upset about what was happening right now. Ever since I'd left Georgia, ever since I'd left the *Him* my mind still refused to give a name to, the truth of my past had been clamoring against my breastbone, begging to get out and see the sunlight. I'd thought a half-dozen times over the last few days about pulling Calla aside and spilling the whole truth about why I'd come to Fortune Springs.

But something always held me back. Fear, maybe. Or my own pride. Maybe I didn't want to be known as the person to whom bad things were always happening. Maybe I just wanted to escape any way I could—including pretending it just hadn't happened at all.

From my side, Owen leveled a steady look at me.

"Because you want to leave…? Okay. And what, exactly, is that supposed to mean?"

"It means that I think I'm better on my own. I think my *life* would be better on my own. Without anyone to tie me down or complicate things. Without anyone to interfere. Without anyone who could—"

I met his gaze and my breath caught.

When I hesitated, he finished the thought for me. "Hurt you."

"Emotionally or otherwise. Yeah."

"This was one of the things I was afraid of, you know. That people would come into town, take the money and the year of free housing and just leave."

"And now that your worst fears have come true?"

The lightning flashed in the distance; I couldn't help the flinch that gripped me by the spine and shook me from my feet all the way to the hairs on top of my head. It was only when I stopped that Owen continued, but he was kind enough not to pry about whether I was okay.

We both knew I wasn't.

"I don't know. Maybe it's not so bad. Maybe I've been looking at this thing all wrong. The Bride House thing, I mean. Like, what if it shouldn't be about what the town gets out of it, but what they can give?"

"Very progressive of you."

"Clearly, Calla is rubbing off on me through you," he teased.

I managed a smile, but not much else. My mind raced. The inevitable dangled ahead of us, and I waited for him to ask it. To continue the line of questioning he'd started earlier.

The truth wanted out. I just wanted to crawl under the blanket in my arms and hide beneath it forever.

"Does she know what happened to you?" Owen asked, eventually picking up the conversational baton once again. "What brought you here to Fortune Springs?"

"Not specifically. But I think she guessed. I feel like it's written across my face, like anyone who looks at me is going to see what a poor, pathetic little creature I am."

"No one who looks at you sees that. You know what I see when I look at you?"

"A half-drowned rat who barely made it through the rain?"

The flames of the fireplace cast a golden glow across Owen's face, so different to how it had been beneath all of the white-hot, silvered lightning outside. When he spoke, I wanted to believe him. Wanted to defy every lesson I'd learned to the contrary and trust him.

"No. I see someone who's obviously been through a lot, but is still fighting for a better future. You haven't given up. You haven't let anything—or anyone—break you. I don't know what you've been through, and you don't have to tell me if you don't want to, but... when I look at you, your courage is written in every inch of your face."

He didn't call me beautiful. He didn't say that my eyes twinkled like stars or that I possessed all of the superficial qualities he looked for in a woman. Being called courageous meant even more to me than all the compliments in the world combined.

I hadn't ever seen myself as brave. How could I, when I was so busy trying to fend off every shadow and bad memory lurking in the corners of my every waking thought?

The truth was that I *hadn't* been brave for a very, very long time. I'd been a coward. And now, I was just trying to survive. Nothing courageous about that. But still… the heart currently stamping out wildfires in my chest thudded twice as hard at the sincerity in his words. Maybe I wasn't, but he *thought* I was brave. Believed me capable of bravery. And that was beautiful, too. Almost as beautiful as the real thing.

"You're going to be disappointed when I tell you the truth."

"You couldn't ever disappoint me. Come on. Why are you here in Fortune Springs? Why are you afraid of the rain? I want to know you, Virginia. All of you. Even the parts you don't especially care to share with anyone."

A crossroads of my own making sprawled out before me. I could bottle the truth yet again. He'd probably be gracious enough to allow me these secrets. Or… I could go in the opposite direction. Trust him. Tell him the truth. And hope he still cared enough about me after he'd heard it to remain in my life.

I didn't want to lose him. Strange as it was—and as much as I closed off my heart to the outside world—I was beginning to enjoy his company enough that the thought of him turning away from me… it broke something inside the dark, closed-off recesses of my heart.

But there was nothing for it. I needed to tell someone the truth. Might as well be the man with honest eyes and a kind smile.

"Alright. You asked for it."

Bracing myself, I collected all the pieces of that courage he'd talked about a moment ago, and tried to force myself to tell everything. From the beginning.

"So, I grew up very poor. The rain didn't bother me back then. My dad split the scene when I was very, *very* young, and my grand-

parents and mom raised me on this backwoods farm in Georgia.
We kept horses for some *very fine* Atlanta folks. You know the type.
Derby hats on Sundays, polo parties on Saturdays?"

"I haven't ever met the type personally, but I can imagine."

I didn't have to imagine. I could still smell the scent of his
cologne and hear the roar of his voice shaking her skeleton as he
stormed through the house. Goosebumps erupted across my flesh.
A chill that had nothing to do with the rain outside wracked my
entire body.

"Well, growing up with nothing and with no one to keep me
company but the animals, I was obsessed with them. These glowing,
beautiful people who descended on our farm every Saturday.
They were like angels. Too perfect. Too luminous. I knew I wasn't
supposed to, that I was meant to be invisible whenever they came
around, but still, I'd hide behind trees to watch them, just so I could
get a glimpse. I wanted to be them. I wanted them to want me."

Oh, how many hours had I spent, hiding behind trees and
peeking through the gap in the farmhouse curtains, just trying to
get a glimpse of them and their gilt-edged, sun-bathed world? The
women, all so poised and stunning. The men, all so strong and
handsome. All of them, so primped and unattainable. They were
like Gods to me back then, descended and touching the earth for
a few brief moments.

Every time I went back to those days, *He* was the first person I
thought about. The first and the last. The Alpha and Omega in this
pantheon of the gods of Georgia.

"There was one in particular, of course, that I especially cared
about. His name was Porter Zachariah Hampton the Third. And

when we were twelve, we got caught in a rainstorm just like this one, and he kissed me. The family found out, of course, and they stopped bringing him around to the farm. But I never forgot that one magical, precious moment."

All this time, I'd been staring into the flames, as if they were some kind of portal into my past. I liked it that way, not giving my attention to Owen. No matter how he looked at me—with pity, with anger, with condescension or understanding—I would probably cry. And the last thing I wanted was to cry.

This was my life. These were the decisions I'd made and the decisions of others that had affected me. Crying wasn't going to change anything. Tears couldn't wash away what had happened, no matter how much I wished that they would.

"Years later, I decided I didn't want to live on the farm anymore. I was going to be independent. To take the world by storm. So, I got a partial scholarship to a school in Savannah and spent the rest of my time working at a catering company. Got through undergrad, not a problem. But then, I went to grad school. And met Porter again. Years later. When I *literally* ran into him at a fundraiser. Him in white tie and tails. Me in my catering outfit, and an incident with red wine that got me fired. He asked to take me out to dinner that night as an apology."

"And?"

One word punctuated by an invisible question mark. A question that had so many answers. Images flashed through my mind, all possibilities for my reply. *And we went to dinner and he told me I had always been so beautiful. And he told me I didn't need that crummy catering job, I was too good for it. And he asked me about money, if I was doing okay. And we started going out and he always seemed so*

*sincere and he always seemed so caring—or was it controlling—and he
said he loved me but always after he'd just gotten something he wanted
and, and, and, and…*

"And it's the same as any sad story goes. I fell in love with him.
And he had the money and the charm and the power and the
influence to get me to do whatever he wanted."

"Did he love you?"

Another question with too many answers. A riddle I'd driven
myself half-mad in those last few weeks with him trying to solve.

"I don't know." My voice broke. The tears threatened. I'd given
myself over to a man I didn't even know loved me. I'd missed every
red flag and every warning sign. He'd been a monster, lurking in
the shadows and waiting to show me his true form. "I really don't.
Maybe in the beginning he did, but after that, he… I think he liked
having someone he could control. Someone who needed him more
than he needed her."

"What did he do?"

So many things. Too many things. I decided to just go with the
highlight reel, the pieces and parts of me that still stuck around
after all of this time away from him.

"Oh, got me to drop out of my master's program and stay home
to look after his house. Got me to stop eating so I'd look better when
we went out to parties and dinners and *events* together. But even
that wasn't enough. It wasn't enough to control my every waking
moment." A phantom pain scraped across my left cheek, as fresh
and as sharp as if the memory were happening again in real life.
"After all of that time, I felt like a stranger to myself. Like I was
watching my life instead of living it."

There was no more delaying the heart of the matter. The hardest thing to put into words. If I could have held it back, I would have. But I'd almost confessed everything. No going back now.

"The first time he hit me... it was like a wake-up call. He cried and said he was sorry and told me he'd never do it again, but that whole night, I stayed awake plotting and planning and organizing my thoughts to leave him. That was the night I found out about the Bride House. It felt like fate. And I don't even *believe* in fate. But I don't know... it felt like the place was calling me. Offering an escape. And that's what I did. I escaped."

Not easily, of course. And straining against the mental cords he'd implanted in my brain hadn't been easy, either. Ridiculous thoughts hounded me with every step I took away from him. *You'll be sorry. You are never going to get someone that good-looking ever again. Or someone that rich. Or someone that smart. One day, you'll regret that you didn't stay. That you didn't make a few sacrifices for a life most women would kill to have.*

Those thoughts still haunted me sometimes. I still hadn't been able to snip those last few invasive wires he'd managed to wire through me.

Owen was silent for a long time. I could practically hear the gears turning in his head. He was staring, but not really seeing anything. "And he just let you go?"

"I left while he was at work and tossed my phone in a garbage can in Mississippi. I don't know how he reacted. All I know is that the whole bus ride to Fortune Springs, I just kept thinking about my freedom. About *finally* being free after years and years of that prison of a relationship. I figured I would go to Fortune Springs, pass go, collect my money, and take the first ride I could to get out to California, where I could buy a little shack on the beach and never see another living soul ever again if I didn't want to. Where I could wake up every morning and taste my freedom on the wind."

"But now, you're not so sure you want that anymore?"

The call-out was so direct, so abrupt, I almost let my subconscious answer for me. *No, I'm not so sure at all.* Somehow, I managed to catch myself, though, before my real, unfiltered answer made it out there.

"I like it here in Fortune Springs. Or, I'm starting to. But I want my freedom. That hasn't changed."

"But belonging to people, caring about them and letting them care about you, that's not a prison. That's one of the best things about being free. You finally get to choose who you let in. Who gets to love you, not who gets to control you." He paused. "I know I can never understand what you're going through or what you've been through. And I understand why you don't want to trust people or let them in. But I hope… I hope one day, everyone here can earn your trust. I hope *I* can earn that trust."

For the first time since I'd started my story, I peered at him from the corner of my eye. I couldn't help but wonder what *he* was hiding beneath all of those gruff layers of firefighter exterior.

"What about you? Do you let people love you?"

"I haven't been very good at it lately, no. We all have our own reasons to escape to Fortune Springs."

I processed this piece of news. Owen, the steadfast defender of this little town, wasn't even from here. I could tell, though, that now wasn't the time for detailed follow-up questions. "Will you tell me about it some day? What brought you to this town?"

"Yeah. Someday."

The lightning flashed again. Then, thunder rattled the windows on their hinges. My shoulders shook despite the warmth of the fire.

"You know, you never told me why you don't like thunderstorms."

"Because when it rained, he drank. And when he drank, things got worse."

Like the warmth of the fire, his warmth felt closer than ever. Just at my side, far enough to be polite and close enough that I could feel his hum of quiet, controlled energy. I had another choice, another crossroads, this one smaller than the others. I could continue to sit here on my own, or I could close the small, inches-wide gap between them, and rest on him.

My muscles began to unwind, relaxing slowly back into his arms. He didn't say anything when I got there, only kept me in his loose but contented grip as we stared out the window together, watching the patterns dance upon the thick cut-glass window pane.

"You know… I don't think I've ever just sat down and watched a thunderstorm before. It's actually kind of beautiful," I said.

More time passed. Hours? Minutes? I didn't know. All I knew was that, eventually, I had my head on his chest, and my eyes were getting terribly, terribly heavy. More thunder. Louder, this time. I yawned instead of flinching this time.

"The storm's getting worse."

I could practically hear Owen's simple, small smile in his voice. "Well, good thing is, this little shack isn't going anywhere."

And neither am I, his heartbeat seemed to say.

*

As they were wont to do, the storm passed. Eventually, Owen and I were forced from our little place of seclusion and back outside, where the real world waited for us, with all of its complications, its problems, and its promise.

In the same way I'd never much looked at a storm before, when I stepped out of the cabin that evening, I realized I'd never taken much notice of the moments *after* a storm either. Out there, by the lake, with the sun peeking out silver and gold behind the dark, scattering clouds, the entire valley filled with stray streams of priceless beauty. After the darkness and the cold and the danger of the storm, life peeked out from every corner. The colors of the green grass and the blue water were deeper, somehow. They weren't just green and blue anymore. The flowers weren't just sparks of purple amongst the weeds and the earth. Everything took on jewel tones. Emerald. Sapphire. Amethyst. The diamond sky filled with crystalline light. The copper ground radiated beneath them with ruby warmth. The fresh air tasted butter rich on my tongue, making me hungry for something I couldn't quite name.

Owen wasn't a stranger anymore, either. He now knew the truth about me, a truth I'd finally acknowledged out loud—not all of it, anyway—and he hadn't left. He hadn't run away. He'd held me, helping me keep the broken pieces of myself together until the storm passed. And as we stood there, I realized that I was closer than ever before to falling. Falling into life here in Fortune Springs. Falling into something new. Falling for him.

Chapter Seventeen

I tried to go back to my normal, small town, Bride House life. After my tour around town and the lock-in at the lake, though, that proved completely impossible. There was no *normal* for me now. There was only *new*. I'd fought so hard and sacrificed so much to escape being the girl that bad things happened to, and now, I'd branded myself in front of the one person I wanted to see me as strong and capable. He hadn't let on that he thought less of me now—exactly the opposite, actually—but still, my insecurities nagged at me, forcing me to stay up at all hours of the night and examine every new memory I made with him, searching and scanning his remembered face for any signs I may have originally missed.

I didn't find any. And I didn't shy away from him. As hard as it was, I took some guidance from the little plants outside in the front yard, the ones Calla had been devoting so much of her time and energy to in recent days. She'd propped them up with small contraptions of stick and wire, forcing them to grow up towards the sun.

I was doing the same thing, really. Forcing myself not to run away. Not to die. To grow towards the sun. And one such afternoon, as I struggled to finish my entrance essay with a lap full of puppies fighting for my attention, I waited for Owen to arrive and collect them.

Calla was out in the garden. Tending to those same little plants. Adjusting them as necessary.

"How's it going down there?" I asked, when she appeared on the porch to take a long swig from her travel mug of iced coffee.

"Oh, it's growing."

A pun that bad totally deserved the chuckle and eye-roll I gave it. "Great."

Not to be undone by someone critiquing her sense of humor, Calla adjusted her sunglasses. "But I should be asking you. How are things going up there?"

"Fine. Why?"

"It's just interesting, is all," she said, her voice pitching up into a tone that promised she was *not* as casual as she tried to seem. "First time I've ever seen you wear makeup."

My breathing stopped, just for the briefest of seconds, just long enough for someone to notice. Was that true? Had I really not worn makeup while here in Fortune Springs? And was it really so obvious? An unconvincing lie bubbled to my throat. "I've worn makeup before."

"Is that true?"

I didn't answer. I'd already lied once. Calla barked a good-natured laugh.

"Excited about your firefighter coming over?"

"He's not my firefighter."

"Do you want him to be?"

The papers in my lap fluttered in the wind; the puppies mewled and cooed. I wanted nothing more than to return to them and pretend that this conversation never happened. "I don't know how to answer that."

"A simple yes or no would suffice. Or, if you're not sure how you feel about him, you could do some more research. Put that makeup to good use."

Calla's stare turned knowing and almost triumphant. That usually spelled trouble for me. "What are you thinking, Calla? I don't like that look on your face."

"You could go to Gold Teeth Pete's. Saloon here in town. Invite him if you want to see what he's like outside the Fire House."

"I don't know—"

"Or, if you don't want to go with him, why don't you go on your own? Might be a good, new way to stretch yourself. Get yourself out there."

"Yeah. Maybe. I'll think about it."

"Well, don't take too long to think about it. Here comes your Prince Valiant."

The only way she could have seen him before me was from the reflection in the glass windows lining the facade of the house, but sure enough, when I turned, there he was, walking up the front path towards us. When his eyes met mine, I could have sworn his smile got bigger.

"Hey, Virginia," he called, closing the final space between himself and the porch. "Calla, good to see you."

"Hm. Speak for yourself," the woman replied, her lips a thin line that wholly gave away the soft spot she was trying hard to conceal.

"I'm so glad we can share these moments together, m'am."

"Virginia," Calla sighed, ignoring him altogether now, "I'll see you later. I'm going to look at the flowers in the backyard."

The hasty exit probably had more to do with giving Owen and I more time alone together than any pressing matter in the currently barren backyard, but we let her go anyway. As she left, I knew I had a decision to make, but rather than over-analyzing it, I tried to just let my gut speak for me.

And I tried not to think about the wave of hope currently filling my body with sunshine.

"Thanks for looking after the puppies," Owen said, picking Pike up with gentle hands and slipping him into one of the oversized pockets of his seasonally inappropriate coat. Where I loved to take the pups on long walks with their six-lined leash, Owen preferred to walk around with pockets full of puppies for convenience. "With all the guys over at the Fire House for our meeting, I didn't want them getting overexcited."

"No worries," I said, smiling broadly. "Hey, I'm thinking about going to Gold Teeth Pete's tonight. They tell me that's where all the fun happens in this town."

Something strange flickered in Owen's eyes. Something dark. It didn't worry me, but it did leave me curious, especially when he only followed up with a noncommittal: "Oh, yeah?"

"I mean, I don't really drink, but I thought maybe it could be fun. Do a little bit of line dancing or whatever it is wannabe cowboys do when they go to bars."

"Are you sure? Gold Teeth Pete's can get a little... rough."

He practically winced on the last word. Calla hadn't said anything about the place being that way. Besides, if he went with me, I wouldn't have anything to worry about. "I can't keep hiding, right? I've got to go out and try to live my life, don't I?"

The real question at work there hung in the warm, dry air. It crackled, flame-like, its light dancing between us as I waited for him to answer it. *Do you want to come with me?* Instead of answering it, though, he collected the last of the puppies and stopped even trying to meet my gaze.

"Yeah. Yeah, you do. Well, I hope you have a good time."

"Thanks."

"I've got to get the pups back home."

After the rejection that wasn't really a rejection at all because I'd been too afraid to open my stupid mouth and even ask him if he wanted to go with me, I considered not going. I considered having dinner with Calla and Willa, proposing a long game of Monopoly, and going to bed with a cup of hot chocolate the size of my head.

But Calla had been right when she said, what felt like a lifetime ago, that I couldn't let my past control my future. I couldn't let anyone *from* my past control it, either. I needed to start making my own decisions, needed to start trying new experiences and living the one life I had.

And Gold Teeth Pete's was part of that journey.

The saloon stood at the far edge of town, nestled on a street corner near the mountain—I still hadn't learned the mountain's name or what the range was called… Owen had forgotten that part of his tour—so it could be conveniently accessed by both the loggers coming down from work or anyone who needed a quick après-ski drink after a long day on the slopes. Like the rest of the buildings in the heart of Fortune Springs, it had been built by sturdy frontiersmen, with wood that would outlast and outlive them all. The towering ceilings—leading to a second floor that once housed travelers and working women alike—told me that this wasn't just some new conversion. This had *always* been a saloon, ready to water and entertain the weary folks of the road. Wooden card tables filled what might once have been a dance hall, and a long, mirror-walled bar ran along the western wall of the first floor. An old jukebox played too-loud music.

The bar was flooded with—mostly male, mostly burly, mostly incredibly terrifying in that easygoing, *I'm not here for a good time, not a long time* kind of way—patrons, so I stuck to the corner of the bar, where I could keep my back to the wall and have a full view of the place.

That didn't stop guys from staring. Most of them stayed well enough away, thankfully, but as I slowly sipped my syrupy soda on the rocks—with a cherry and orange slice topper, courtesy of the bartender who laughed in my face the first time I ordered "straight mixer" from him—I couldn't avoid the feeling of their eyes on my shoulders, my hips, the curve of my neck.

I tried to think of this night as exposure therapy. I'd wanted it to be a date with Owen, but in the absence of that, I'd decided that instead of backing down and hiding in my room, I'd let tonight be useful. Instructive.

After all, if I wanted to enjoy my life, I had to actually go out and live it, didn't I?

Whatever I thought about it, though, flew from my mind when a flowery, sugary cocktail was placed in front of me at the bar. When I protested, the bartender told me someone else had bought it for me.

My stomach rolled. That wasn't a good sign.

Sliding the drink away from me as calmly and subtly as I could, I returned to my soda and kept my eyes on the rerun of a baseball game currently playing on a television mounted in the corner. Maybe if I seemed disinterested, unavailable, no one would come asking after that drink they'd bought me.

A vain wish. I should have known better. I should have known men better by now.

"Hey, darlin'. I bought you that drink."

"I don't drink," I said, not even looking towards the gruff, cigarette-roughened voice beside me. His body pressed uncomfortably close to mine, despite the fact that there was plenty of room in this corner of the bar. Nicotine and whiskey wafted off of him in thick clouds, threatening to choke me. I took another sip of my soda.

"What's that in your hand, then?"

"Just a soda. That's all."

"You're just waiting for some other guy to bring you a drink, huh? I'm not good enough for you."

Against my better judgment, pride turned my head in his direction. I was rewarded with a view of a generalized handsome white man who could have been perfectly at home on the cover of any country album or Wrangler commercial. However, there was something sunken and unfocused about his eyes. A sort of rot from the inside that shone through his slightly rough skin.

"That's—"

"No, I understand. You're too good for me. I knew that before I came over here. Or you could prove me wrong. Just by drinking some Sex on the Beach."

A knot of bile rose up in the back of my throat. What a creep. But all of my life's experience taught me that you never fought a bully. You diffused the situation. Backed down until they got bored. It was the best way to keep yourself safe.

"Thank you for the drink," I said, smiling a grit-toothed smile before turning back to the baseball game. A moment passed. Then, two. He didn't move. His oppressive presence hovered over to my left, pressing in dangerously against me. Too close. He was too close to me and I was too close to the wall. A recipe for disaster. Heat ran up the back of my neck.

"But you aren't going to drink it?"

"I don't drink," I said with as much of a smile as I could muster. "I already said that."

"You're in the wrong place if you don't drink alcohol."

"Believe me, I know I'm in the wrong place right now," I muttered.

That's when his hands started to wander. When his boots turned and his legs began marching me back, back, back, until I was pinned against the wall. Fingers dug into my hip. His breath beat against my ear, hard and fast and clouding my senses. His body pinned mine. "Why'd you come here if you weren't going to be friendly? We're all pretty friendly here, least you could do is return the favor."

My fight or flight instincts kicked in, but I wasn't a fighter and I had nowhere to escape to as his breath descended closer and closer to me. I wanted to raise my fists, to do *something* to send this guy packing, but my mind filled with memories and half-remembered feelings, all complicating my need to get the hell out of here.

But then... A voice rose over the din of the bar. A familiar voice. Warm and rugged and usually slightly annoyed with me. Now, it was impossibly stern. The voice of a leader. Of a protector.

Owen Harris.

"What in hell is going on here?"

The man currently pinning me to the wall barely broke his concentration. His hand tightened at my hip, though. His only noticeable sign of distress. "We're just having a good time. You can move right along."

Owen's voice was low, dangerous. And when I managed to turn my gaze in his direction, he looked the part, too. All the attention of this corner of the saloon had turned squarely on them, but he wore the attention well, never taking his eyes from my face. "She doesn't look like she's having a very good time to me."

"I think she would have spoken up if she was uncomfortable. Wouldn't you, little lady?" He didn't give me a chance to respond before returning his attention to Owen, whose hands hung taut and shaking at his sides. "Now, I suggest you run along."

"Funny. I was just thinking the same about you."

"Listen," the guy said with a low, growling laugh. His hand moved lower on my hip, backwards towards the wall and the swell of my ass. Vomit rose up in the back of my throat. "You want a piece, you're going to have to wait your turn."

"Alright. That's enough."

Everything happened quickly then. Owen lunged. The men at the table scattered, leaving the man completely defenseless. Brutal and swift, Owen wrenched him away, finally freeing me to scramble out from my corner…

And out onto the bar floor where, quickly behind me, Owen was pounding the man into the hard wood beneath.

The bar's entire crowd circled now, all cheering on Owen or screaming at him to get away. My heart raced. I wanted nothing more than to dissolve into the floor at that very moment, but something about the way he moved rooted me to the spot. He was vicious, as if he'd been a caged animal finally unleashed back into the wild.

But when the first strands of blood went flying onto the floor, and I couldn't hold back my scream, Owen's trance shattered. He was so brutal, so strong. So destructive. A dozen memories flashed across my mind, each one more triggering than the last. Bolting to his feet, he stared down at the bloody man beneath him, then to the crowd, and then… right to me.

His eyes were a mixture of pain and regret, of worry and wonder. I didn't know how to decode such a mixture of expressions and sensations. My own heart, too, was just as confusing as his stare. I was equal parts grateful and terrified.

I'd always seen the promise of violence in his rippling muscles and imposing figure. But now, I'd seen that promise kept in all its bloody glory. His knuckles were dripping red now. A silent threat and promise.

"I…" His mouth hung open. No one seemed to know what to do, what to say. Least of all him. "I didn't mean—I've got to go."

The crowd parted for him, and within a moment, he was gone.

My stomach pitched. Everyone was going to be talking about this tomorrow. Calla would probably know all of the sordid details by the time I got home tonight.

But strangely, knowing that this would be the hot gossip by sunrise didn't disturb me half as much as realizing that I was falling in love with a man who could leave a stranger a bloody, broken pulp on a barroom floor.

Somehow, I managed to stumble back to the Bride House, where the lights were on, waiting for me. Calla was always good about that—making her home a welcoming oasis in the darkness—and the second I made it through the front door, I relished the familiar sounds and smells and feelings of being back home. Slamming the door behind me, I leaned against it and closed my eyes, grateful for a minute of peace. A peace that was quickly interrupted by a lazy, almost distracted little voice.

"Hi, Virginia."

My eyes snapped open, and through the open French doors to the living room, I saw Willa curled up in one of the big, worn leather chairs, reading a book under the light of a lamp bigger than she was.

At this point, I was practically starving for a distraction from my own thoughts and feelings. Walking into the living room, I gave her all of my attention. Well, most of my attention. It was split between speaking to her and trying to keep myself from giving away that anything was wrong.

"Hey, kiddo. What are you still doing up?"

Without looking up from the pages, she held up a library paper-wrapped tome. "I've only got a few more pages left in this chapter."

I checked the clock. Way past her bedtime. "You've got school in the morning. Scoot. Time for bed."

"Alright."

She was on her feet too quickly, and agreeing way too readily. I chuckled under my breath. Did she think I was born yesterday?

"And no reading with your flashlight under the covers."

"How did you know I was going to do that?"

"I was a kid once, too. I know all the tricks."

With that, I sank into the nearest chair, taking my weight off of my unsteady legs. I loved these moments with Willa, the ones where I felt like part of a real family. I wanted to cling on to them with everything I had, but as soon as I heard her padding out of the room, my previous war returned inside of my heart.

A little voice broke my train of thought. "Are you okay, Virginia? You don't look so good."

No, I supposed I didn't. Not that I would know for sure. I wasn't brave enough to check myself in the nearby mirror. It was currently taking all of my energy not to unload all of the soda in my stomach onto the hardwood floor.

"Yeah. I'm just…" I should have known better than to say what I said next. But bitterness consumed me. Resentment and pain and frustration. It all flooded out of me before I could stop myself. "I'm just remembering that maybe it's better to be invisible, you know. Just try to survive instead of thrive. It's easier that way."

Swallowing hard, I put on a brave smile. I was the grown-up in this situation, after all. It wasn't my place to dump my problems onto some poor kid.

"But don't worry about me. I just had a bad day. Just like *you'll* have a bad day tomorrow if you don't get upstairs and go to sleep, posthaste."

"Goodnight," she said.

"Goodnight," I replied.

But I knew I wasn't going to be having a good night. It would be a miracle if my racing mind allowed me to sleep at all.

Chapter Eighteen

The next day, I didn't even attempt to leave my room. Living off glasses of water from my bathroom tap and a stale granola bar from the bottom of my backpack, I burrowed under the covers and tried to flip through some of the books I'd borrowed on one of mine and Willa's many recent library trips.

That didn't help. Neither did the blazing sunshine outside of my window, which seemed to mock my mood with its warmth and beauty.

Once, I heard Calla's familiar, slightly offbeat footsteps walk to my bedroom door, but after a moment of hesitation, she continued walking down the stairs, leaving me in peace.

Good. That was what I wanted.

Wasn't it?

No, I definitely didn't want to talk about my growing feelings for Owen… or the terror I felt after last night's display. I didn't want to unburden myself of these conflicting emotions and I *definitely* didn't want Calla's guidance on what I should do next.

My instincts told me that Owen would never hurt me the way he'd hurt that man. That he was a protector, not a bully or a menace. Experience, though, warned me against ever seeing him again.

Doubts about my own judgment clouded my every thought. The voice in my head that sounded so much like Porter's told me that I was doomed, that I'd always fall into facsimiles of the same broken relationship I'd left behind in Georgia.

Once again, I found myself paralyzed by choice. So, instead of choosing, I sat in bed all day, pretending that life wasn't going on outside of my window. That the sounds and the breathing of this quiet, empty house were all there was to the universe.

That was easier than actually reckoning what had happened yesterday.

The world, of course, wasn't content to be ignored for long. Eventually, the house echoed with the sounds of the first-floor telephone ringing. And ringing. And ringing.

Then, it stopped.

Only to start up again almost immediately.

"Calla?" I called, not leaving my bed. "Calla, the phone is ringing."

Calla didn't answer. Neither me, nor the telephone. A twinge of fear raced through me. What if it was Owen calling? What if he wanted to talk to me? What would I even say?

The silence of the house didn't last for long. The damned ringing started again. Throwing the covers off of my bed, I threw on a sweater and some slippers before treading quickly down the stairs. I missed that last call, but as soon as I reached the landing of the staircase, the ringing started again.

They were persistent, this caller. And they stayed on the line until I reached the receiver and picked it up, forcing myself to answer in as strong a voice as I could manage. "Hello, the Bride House. Who may I ask is calling?"

"Calla, is that you?"

I didn't recognize the voice on the other end of the line. I was so grateful that it wasn't Owen, I didn't even care who it was, really.

"No, sorry, this is Virginia. Calla is out, I think. I don't know when she'll be back. Can I take a message?"

"Ah, sorry," the voice said, immediately rushing with something like relief. "It's Principal Hernandez, calling from Willa's school. You don't know when Calla is coming back?"

"No, sir."

"Hm. Well. You were the one who got her into school. Would you accept responsibility as her temporary guardian?"

My fingers clenched the phone receiver even tighter than before. If they needed a parent or legal guardian and they'd called this many times, it probably wasn't because Willa had forgotten to get a permission form signed.

"Uh, yeah. Sure. Of course. Is everything okay? Did something happen?"

A pause on the other end of the line. The old phone wires crackled as I waited for his answer. "I think you should come down to the school. As soon as possible, if you don't mind."

"Sure. I'll be right over."

I was positive that, on my walk over to the county school, everyone who passed me on the street stared as I went. Not just because I was racing like a bat out of hell, but also because of the stories that no doubt seeped out of Gold Teeth Pete's about last night. But I didn't see them. I didn't care about the whispers or the looks. All I could think about was the fear of unknowing, of not being told what had happened with Willa at the school. My vision tunneled until I arrived there and followed the printed placards leading me up the front, concrete steps and into the high school office.

This wasn't like me. I wasn't assertive or bold. I didn't often stand up for myself, not unless it was absolutely necessary. My previous relationship had basically beaten the fight out of me. But when it came to Calla and Willa, when it came to the woman who'd given me a home and her granddaughter who'd given me her friendship, that fight resurfaced. They were so important to me that the past didn't matter anymore. My fear didn't matter anymore.

I cared about them more than I cared about myself.

So, when I threw open the glass and metal doors of the school's front office and I saw Willa sitting there in a bloody T-shirt, holding an ice pack to her bruised and pulped face, my entire world went red. A rage the likes of which I'd never known before flooded me, and I turned on the principal standing by the front desk, not caring for formalities or niceties and letting that rage guide me wherever it wanted to go.

This wasn't the first time I'd seen a reflection of myself in this girl. But this was the first time I wanted to make someone else hurt as much as they'd made her hurt.

"What the *hell* happened here?"

"Well," the principal said, clearing his throat and adjusting his tie as he did so. "We don't really know."

An incredulous laugh escaped me. Bitter. Harsh. Jagged. "You don't know? You can't take one look at her and see what happened?"

When he didn't answer me, I turned to her. The bruising was extensive on her face and arms. Her ponytail had been dislodged as though someone had been pulling on it. Dried, crusty blood made small mountains around her nose and mouth. Surprisingly, though, I didn't have the urge to retch. Instead, I had the urge to smash.

"Willa, are you okay?"

Wide, brown eyes looked up at me, then returned to a spot on the floor. She didn't say anything or even acknowledge that I'd spoken beyond that. A big, firm hand touched my shoulder blades, and I allowed the principal to take me behind the secretary's desk for some veil of privacy. He lowered his voice.

"She won't tell us what happened. There was a fight in the hallway, and we have the other girls in the next room, but we do know that she didn't fight back."

I would have been less shocked if he'd slapped me. She hadn't even fought back?

"What?"

"The other girls don't have a scratch on them. She just took it."

My voice lowered, the chilling sound surprising even me. "What kind of school are you running here?"

"I'm sorry. Really. I am. This isn't something that happens here—"

"And it better not happen again, you understand me?" The rage was almost tangible now, so real and so close it was practically using me as its puppet. "Oh, you'd better be so glad it's me who came here to get her and not Calla. I'm taking her home for the rest of the day."

"Absolutely. She needs to rest. We'll take care of disciplining the other girls."

"You'd better."

Minutes later, we were out on the sidewalks of Fortune Springs, walking home at an almost painfully slow rate. I matched Willa's pace, not wanting to rush her—not with her walk, not with her story. But when we reached a block away from the house with no word from her, I knew she would probably need a tiny nudge to get going.

"You know," I said, in a soft, understanding tone. "We're going to need to talk about it."

Her boots shuffled along the pavement, kicking up rocks as she dragged them beneath her. No response. Since we'd left the school, my rage had subsided, ebbing into something like a quiet, contained sense of injustice.

"I know you don't want to, but that's just the way it is, alright?" I said, my voice still soft and understanding. "What happened back there? The principal told me you didn't fight back."

Her face went red—a feat considering there were so few parts of her not already purpling with bruises or splotchy red and brown with dried blood. She'd had to give her ice up when we left the office, so already the swelling was beginning to show. My heart went out to her. I understood exactly how she felt right now. I'd been in her position before.

"Willa." I stopped at the gate to the Bride House, putting my hand on the wrought iron to keep her from pushing past me. "You know you're not in trouble, right? I just want to make sure you're okay."

"I am," she muttered, quiet as the wind. "I'm okay."

"Really? Because you look like you went twelve rounds with a heavyweight champion."

My weak attempt at humor, at opening her up, absolutely did not work. If anything, she tucked herself deeper inside, clutching her backpack straps as if for dear life. With surprising deftness and strength for a kid her size and age, she managed to wrench the gates open and march towards the Bride House as if it were some secret home base where she could be immune from my questions and from the strain of the day.

If I were her, I would have done the exact same thing. The Bride House had become a kind of refuge for me, too. But I wasn't going to let her get away so easily. Not after this. Not after today. Following as close behind her as I could, I continued the conversation she clearly didn't want to have.

"Listen, I've been there, kid. I've been… the punching bag." She stopped at the foot of the steps. Knowing I'd gotten her attention, I continued, gaining one step on her so I could look down at her and capture her eyes as I spoke. "Believe me. Telling someone about it makes things a hell of a lot easier."

I knew that from firsthand experience. Telling Owen about my past had been one of the most freeing experiences of my life. The memory of it stung now, but at the time, it had been so beautiful.

Several cars passed on the street beyond the gates before Willa finally collapsed to the first step. Her legs just gave out.

"You told me that it was better just to take it. Just to be invisible. So, that's what I did. Those girls were making fun of me, but I didn't say anything. That made them mad. And they started to hit me. I thought… I thought if I just went limp, maybe they'd get bored and leave me alone. And maybe I could get through my time at this new stupid school without too much trouble."

Oh God. My own legs gave out this time. I'd… I'd *taught* her to do this. Through what I'd said and what I'd done during my time at the Bride House, I'd taught another little girl to do the same thing I'd done for so long—let the world beat us down into nothing.

Last night, when I'd come home and told her it was better to be invisible, I'd sealed the deal. This wasn't her fault. She was a child from a bad home who'd only had this awful worldview confirmed by me. This was *my* fault. I should have been a better teacher. Damn the consequences. Damn my fears. I should have been better. If not for my own sake, than for hers.

I should have taught her it was never okay to let a human being treat another human being like that. Such a small, basic thing. And I'd failed.

"Willa." She didn't budge. My voice went firm and kind all at once. "Stop. Look at me. Please."

I waited the interminable moments until she finally bucked up the courage to look me in the eye. Then, I held her gaze as I tried to put into words the conviction currently beating down on my conscience.

"I was wrong. Alright? You do not take *any* cruelty from anyone. It isn't better to live your life invisible. This is the one life you've got. The one chance you have to live and enjoy yourself. You do *not* let yourself become a doormat. Not for anything. Not for anyone. Do you understand me?"

"But you said—"

"I was wrong. And I've been a terrible example." A dead chuckle escaped me. Drawing my knees into my chest, I stared into the distance, hating myself for what I'd done. What I'd allowed to happen. "You know, I hid in my room today because I was afraid to face people. What does that teach you? That it's okay to hide from your problems and your feelings? God, I'm such a bad friend."

Dropping my forehead against my knees, I tried with everything in me to ward off the sickening guilt currently turning my stomach. I didn't *deserve* to be free of the guilt, of course, but if I was going to keep helping her through this moment, I needed to sort myself out, too.

Neither of us spoke at first. Companionable silence descended. But then, she said something that shocked me to my core, rattling the very foundations of who I was as a person. Changing everything.

"You know," she said, slightly shuffling her feet against the chipping paint of the bottom step, "everyone at school thinks you're my big sister."

"Why do they think that?"

"I might have told them it was true."

My heart clenched, painfully and beautifully. I'd… I'd never been a big sister before. Never had someone look up to me. Even more powerful than that, though, was that we weren't sisters by blood. She'd chosen me.

And I'd failed her.

In that moment, I knew that things had to change. *I* had to change. No more hiding. No more cowering. No more half-assed trying at this thing called life. No more running away.

The truth was, I loved Willa like she was my own sister, too. I'd never had one before, but instinctually, I knew that this was the feeling of it. To care about someone so much you'd finally take the leap away from every bad thing you'd ever known and been, just to help them find a better future for themselves.

"Well, then. I've been a terrible big sister. But tell you what. If I try to change, you've got to try, too. Stand up for yourself. Try to go out and make some friends. Enjoy your new, stupid school."

"But what if they don't like me? What if I look like an idiot, trying to stand up for myself? What if…" She looked down at her scratched-up palms. The wounds were fresh. Jagged. "What if I'm just not good at it?"

I'd been there once before. Believing I would fail before I'd even tried. So, I gave her the same advice Calla had given me. The same advice I now needed more than ever.

"But what if you *are?*"

That hung in the air. And for the first time today, Willa granted me a tiny, almost imperceptible smile. It wasn't much. But it was a start.

"Come on. Let's go inside and get something frozen for your face. And while we're in the freezer, we might as well get some ice cream, too."

"That sounds good to me."

We spent the rest of the night tending to her slightly busted-up face, and explaining to Calla why it wouldn't be a good idea for her to "go down to that school of yours and give them a piece of my mind." My own fight completely forgotten, we spent the night on the couch, eating pizza from the town's only delivery spot and watching reruns of some sitcom until our sides hurt from laughing. Not necessarily because the show was so funny on the seventh or eighth watch, but because we needed the release. We needed to laugh again.

But in the lulls of quiet space between the laughter and the television-supplied quips, my mind wandered down the street to

Owen. I'd made a promise to Willa that I would try. That I would no longer lie down and let the world walk all over me.

My heart told me that Owen was a good decision. That he wasn't like the men in my past. He'd proved that time and time again. And I wouldn't know if my heart was a good judge of character unless I tried.

Which meant that, first thing tomorrow, I'd be going back to the Engine House. And going right back to Owen.

Chapter Nineteen

The next morning, first thing, I returned Owen's favor and brought along two cups of freshly brewed coffee. A peace offering for the barrage of silence I'd given him after the fight at Gold Teeth Pete's. The puppies, who'd been lounging on the front porch with their mother in a patch of sunshine, immediately set upon me the minute I walked through the gate, making it almost impossible to make it to the front door without tripping. Somehow, though, I managed it.

And I was rewarded with Owen Harris' tired, almost haggard-looking face when I arrived.

It reminded me of the first time I'd come to this house; he'd looked worse for wear then, too. Only this time, unlike the last time, I *knew* I was the cause of his distress. His sleepless nights. The bags beneath his eyes.

But I didn't feel bad. I just felt determined. Determined to figure out how I was going to move past today, to figure out whether or not this man was worthy of my trust.

My gut already knew the answer. But I wanted him to look in my eyes and tell me the truth. I wanted him to confirm what my heart was already telling me. I wanted him to wipe away my doubts.

I knew that this would be one of the hardest conversations of my life—the kind that would determine my course going forward. So, of course, I tried to kill the moment with a half-hearted joke, extending one of the two cups in my hand.

"You look like you could use some coffee."

When I'd arrived at Coffeebou and asked for my usual order as well as Owen's, the woman behind the counter had stared at me with the stunned look of a deer about to get hit by a Mack truck. Now, I understood why. Word had gotten around town about the barroom blitz at Gold Teeth Pete's, and the man at the center of it must have been so ashamed that he hadn't even gone in for his usual morning coffee.

He didn't take the coffee from me now, either. I nudged again.

"We've got to stop meeting like this."

No response. His stubbled jaw opened, then closed. A pang went through my chest, another one of the many, many pieces of me trying to say that he wasn't bad. That he wasn't like the other men I'd known in my life. I let out a long, low whistle, but kept the rest of me guarded. If I was wrong, if he was really all that bad, I didn't want him to think he could manipulate me. I needed to be smart about this, needed to be clever about how I went about getting information from him.

"Man, you're really in a bad way, aren't you?"

More time passed. The light fog still clinging to the grass, fighting the onset of the morning, whispered around my ankles. My goosebumps rose and fell before he finally spoke, his voice raw.

"I've wanted to come and see you, but I..." He looked down at his empty hands, flexing them and fisting them as if they weren't truly part of his body. Then, he shoved them into his pockets. "I don't know what to say, really. I feel like everything I come up with is just going to screw things up even worse, somehow."

"I'll be honest," I said, making a promise to him and to myself that would carry us through the rest of this little talk. The hard stuff was always hard to say out loud, but it was always the most important. I couldn't hide from the fact that part of me was afraid of him after what had happened at the bar. The casual ease of his violence. "I don't think things can get that much worse right now."

Instead of addressing the elephant in the room, he surprised me by turning the conversation in a completely different direction.

"I heard Willa got into a scrape at school."

Small towns. Never can keep a secret here, can you? "Yeah, she did. But we talked about it, and she's not going to let anyone do that to her ever again. She's going to be brave. And so am I. It's the reason I'm here."

"For answers."

"Yeah. For answers."

With that one exchange, he must have realized I wasn't going to leave any time soon. I was going to understand what happened the other night, or I was going to sit here until kingdom come. Gently, he took the coffee from my hands. I could tell he was trying to be careful not to let our fingers touch as he did so.

"What questions do you have?"

What questions *didn't* I have? "Just about every one there is. Why didn't you want to go with me that night if you were just going to show up? Were you following me? And that guy… Do you… Do you do stuff like that a lot? And why did you run? Why didn't you stay and talk to me? Why did you leave?"

"'Lotta questions."

"I've had a day and change to think about it. It's just that I was…" Here it was again. That big, difficult truth that I needed to face. "Well, I was really starting to care about you, and—"

"And I ruined it."

No, he didn't ruin it. At least, not *entirely*. There was still a glimmer of hope, one that I was hanging on to as tightly as I could manage.

"And I'm scared," I said. "But I don't think it's fair to just abandon you after everything because I'm scared. I want to understand. I want to understand you."

"I don't really like to talk about myself. About anything serious, really. It's the Fortune Springs way. We're all very tight-lipped around here."

Yeah, I'd noticed that. The town was an oyster in that way. Hard to crack, but filled with treasure once you managed it. Fortune Springs had never lost its frontier spirit—that belief that they *could* make it on their own… but it would be plenty nice if they didn't *have* to make it on their own. I persisted.

"How did you come to be in Fortune Springs, anyway? You aren't from here, right?"

"No, I'm not."

A pause. I waited. So did he.

"That's it?" I finally asked. "*That's* the answer?"

He let out a long sigh and finally moved from the frame of the doorway. Moving to the front porch swing, he left plenty of space for me to come and sit next to him, but I think we both knew I wasn't going to do that. Not just yet anyway. Leaning back against one of the posts of the porch, I kept my distance and waited for him to reply.

"Yep. That's the answer."

"But I want to know. Everything."

"Why? So you'll have an excuse to never have to see me again?"

I flinched, hoping the words and the gesture came out sharper than he'd intended. My voice hardened. My determination to get through to him rose with every wall and defense he tried to put up. I recognized this evasion from my textbooks and my case studies. He was hiding from me, trying to keep me from seeing too deeply into him. Classic behavior. "I'm here with you now. That must mean I'm willing to hear you out."

"Why is that, by the way?"

"Because, believe it or not, I actually like you. And I want to understand you."

There I was—throwing his own words from the cabin back in his face. Not cruelly or maliciously, of course, but because I knew it was the best way to get under his skin. He blinked, as if he'd awakened from a deep slumber. Or as if the last few minutes hadn't really been him, but some stranger.

"If I tell you the truth, I'm going to lose you. If I don't tell you anything, I'm going to lose you. It's a lose-lose-lose proposition for me on every side."

"Then you might as well tell the truth." I thought back to the cabin again, when I told him about Porter and my past. No one else on Earth knew that much of the truth. If I could handle it, then he certainly could, too. "I've told *you* the truth. It's the least you can do."

"I did a bad thing back home," he said after a long pause. Once again, his gaze fell to his hands. That defeated, hurt stare. "And I never wanted to do it again, so I ran."

That was the answer I had been dreading. My chest tightened. The air in my lungs calcified, thickening until it was hard to breathe properly. "What did you do?"

Finally, he pulled himself from the staring contest he'd been having with his own hands, and gave me his full face, tired and worn as it was. I wasn't sure if I hated him or respected him for that. For delivering what followed straight to me. Giving me the whole truth with a side helping of his tortured expression.

"I don't drink anymore, but I used to. A lot. I haven't touched the stuff in years, but back when I was younger and I *did* drink, I would get violent, especially when some guy was roughing up some woman. My dad was not the kindest guy to my mom and, I don't know, I guess it was a trigger for me."

He cleared his throat. "So, this one night, I go outside of the bar in my hometown—a dive, the worst kind of place to drink—to get some fresh air and this guy has a woman pinned to his car. And she's struggling and this haze of red just overtakes me and... And I beat him. Like I've never beaten a person before. He almost died."

His voice cracked. I waited for him to take a long sip of coffee or clear his throat again to cover it up, but he didn't. I watched him bear the weight of his guilt. He didn't want to hide it. He wanted to face it.

Yes, it was definitely respect I felt now.

"The police didn't charge me, but I skipped town all the same. I couldn't handle the person I'd become. Couldn't handle how I'd hurt someone so badly. The guilt ate away at me and... it's still there, picking at the bones."

His voice was gruff now, uncertain and filled with emotion. "I didn't tell you because... I don't know. I guess I wanted you to like me. I wanted you to be able to trust me, and now, I know I won't ever get that."

Shoulders slumped, head bowed, he wordlessly signaled that this was the end of his story. That he'd said everything he could and maybe even more. For my part, I took a long moment to sift through my thoughts and my feelings, a confusing mess of perspectives and worries and hopes.

Yes, he could be dangerous. I'd seen that firsthand. But he wasn't now. He'd done so much to fight for freedom from the worst parts of himself. He was *good*. A kind of goodness I'd maybe never faced before in my entire life.

Strangely, the dominant feeling wasn't about any of that, though. It was about those little words he'd said somewhere in the mix of everything else. *I wanted you to like me. I wanted you to trust me. Now, I won't ever get that.* My heart gave a girlish flutter at the thought of this man wanting me. I knew that was probably the wrong feeling to have in this situation. But with the danger gone, with my trust in him secure, I felt a lightness wash over me. A sense of belonging. Like this could really be the start of the new life I'd hoped coming to Fortune Springs would be.

It was the fulfillment of a promise I'd made to myself, and I couldn't escape the quiet joy that brought me.

"I don't know about that."

"What?"

He blinked up at me as I pushed off the railing against which I'd been leaning for so long.

"You came to Fortune Springs and became a firefighter?"

"Yeah."

"And you haven't…" It had been my intention to sit beside him on the porch swing, but a thought that came to me suddenly made me stop in my tracks. "I mean, until that night at Gold Teeth Pete's, you've never hurt someone like that again?"

"No. Never."

It was so confident, so earnest, that I had no choice but to sit down and move closer to him. "So, you came to this place to learn how to help people. You came to Fortune Springs because you wanted to change. Most people don't ever attempt to get better. But you're here doing the damn thing. I don't know. I don't think you've lost my trust quite yet."

"Really?"

The hope in his voice pierced me straight through. He must not be used to people believing in him. I knew the feeling. We were all such broken people, weren't we? All hoping that someone out there could believe in us. "Yes. Really. You needed a new start, just like I did."

For a long time, we listened to the rusting groan of the porch swing as we allowed the wind to lazily blow us back and forth as it pleased. Peace settled between us, the kind that could only exist between two people who completely and totally trust each other. Between two people who belonged together. But I still had one more question.

"Am I going to be safe with you?"

"Yeah. I promise."

"You want to know something wild?"

"What?"

My head tipped over onto his shoulder. I breathed in his rich, warm scent, letting it fill me as easily and naturally as the wind.

"I actually believe you."

Chapter Twenty

From that day, everything changed. No, not everything. In fact, nothing around me changed, not materially, anyway.

I was the one who changed.

It's hard to describe exactly what happened in the days following my talk with Willa and my reconciliation with Owen. The best way I could think to describe it reminded me of a memory from my childhood. When I was a little girl, I'd gone out into the woods near our house and found an abandoned shack. It might have been a hunting blind at one point, or it might have just been someone's hideaway, but by the time I found it, it was little more than an abandoned structure, aged by the exposure of the forest and the time it had spent unattended.

At that time, I'd been desperate for something that was mine—anywhere I could escape from my home and the ghosts of our family that wasn't. So, slowly, over stolen hours in the afternoon when no one was paying me any attention, I'd slip out of the house and head to my little shack in the woods, where I used things I'd swiped from the house and the barn to fix the old place up. A crowbar to get the warped door open. A rough cloth to wipe away the cobwebs. Some (probably unsafe) cleaner to wipe the grime and signs of wear from the small glass windows set into the walls.

Within days, the dark shack flooded with light and the stale air inside of it cleaned out. It became my refuge, a place to run when I needed to feel the sun on my face while also feeling protected at the same time.

When my mother found it, she had it torn down and used the wood for a bonfire, the kind she often constructed when she wanted to burn up the large pieces of garbage the local trash collectors couldn't handle.

I watched my sunshine house go up into flames that day, but I still remembered the feeling of stepping into that once-dark space and seeing it filled with light. I could still remember the way the dust motes danced through the golden rays, so free and carefree.

That's how it felt for me now. Not like I was *watching* that happen, but like I *was* that small shack. Suddenly full of warmth and sunshine. Aired out. Finally open again.

Everyone and everything contributed to that feeling. The way I wrote my entrance essay for college. Calla spending long after-noons to talk with me on the front porch. Helping Willa with her homework and talking through her days at school.

And, of course, there was Owen. I hadn't had a crush in a long, long time. I hadn't let myself feel anything for a man in almost as long a time. It had always been safer that way. *I'd* always been safer that way. If you didn't feel something for someone, he didn't have the power to hurt you.

Sure, I'd been attracted to him from the start, but that was fine. Anyone could be attractive. This? This was different.

There was no denying my feelings for Owen, not anymore. I felt safe with him. I felt comfortable with him. And more than anything, I felt *happy* with him. Whether we were giving the puppies disastrous baths or just walking down to the town center for a cup of coffee, he always knew exactly what to say to get me to smile, or to change the way I was handling a problem, or to make me laugh until I thought I couldn't breathe anymore.

I didn't know what we were, exactly. We'd never been out on a real *date*—not one we'd ever called a date, anyway—but we'd been together on a lot of things that felt like dates. And I wanted him. I wanted to be with him the way I wanted a cup of coffee in the morning—because it was right. The perfect thing I needed and desired all at once.

I wanted to give something back. I wanted to do something for these people who'd done so much for me. The entire town of Fortune Springs had welcomed me into their homes, their lives, their community, and every day, I found my thoughts drifting to ways I could repay them.

My chance came one afternoon, when Willa came home with a frown on her face and a wrinkle in the center of her forehead. At first, my pulse jumped at the sight of her, but when I confirmed that there weren't any new bruises or scrapes and realized her face was one of contemplation instead of anger or fear, I let my shoulders relax and returned the majority of my focus to the plate of snacks I was knee-deep in assembling.

"What's wrong, kiddo?"

Willa dropped her backpack to the kitchen floor with a marked *thud*. The chair scraped, nails on chalkboard loud, as she pulled it away from the counter to sit. "School thing."

"Yeah?"

That was all the prompting she needed, apparently. I took it as a small victory. When she first moved here, getting her to even answer a question with a shrug or a facial expression was the height of communication. Now, she was stringing together full, overwrought sentences like any other early-years teen. "We have service day coming up next week. They do it at the end of the year to make the students give back or whatever."

"Seems like a good idea."

"And the class with the highest participation—from their class and other people in town—gets to have this big pizza party thing. Everyone wants it, but no one in my class has an idea what we should do. The tenth graders are already going to the animal hospital a couple of counties over. How could we compete with puppies and baby deer?"

I chuckled at that. As someone who spent a pretty significant amount of time every day with puppies, I knew that it was pretty damn near impossible to beat any event in which puppies featured. Handing her a plate of the snacks I'd just prepared—including a few of those little pizza-stuffed pastry squares—I reminded her of one simple, easy fact.

"You know, we could just throw a pizza party."

"It's not the same."

She didn't so much say that as she groaned it, but in the way she dropped her head in her hands, I understood a different dimension to her frustrations. If we just threw a party at the Bride House, it was really a crapshoot, determining whether or not anyone from her class would show up. But if they won a party through school, then *everyone* would be there. It was another bonding experience, another way for her to become part of her community.

I nodded, sagely, as an idea formed.

"Well, I see your predicament. But you were right to come to me."

"Why?"

"Because I happen to know someone who has puppies. And whose Fire House is in desperate need of a paint job. And you know that your grandmother has people who owe her favors all over town."

The trouble wasn't planning the thing. That was easy enough. I pulled a few strings and asked the people I knew around town for some help, and Calla called in nearly every favor she had to get this little event of ours on track. The real trouble was keeping this—especially something as big as this—a secret in a town like Fortune Springs.

Once word got out about what we were doing, we had to keep reminding folks *not* to let word get to Owen. He was a proud man, after all, and I didn't want that pride getting in the way of the good we wanted to do for him.

Also… I kind of wanted to see the look on his face when he saw what we had planned.

When we arrived that morning, everyone was instructed to approach the Fire House as quietly as possible and collect on the front lawn. We'd first gathered in the park near the center of town—the same one where Calla visited the Farmers' Market every week—and it took my breath away, to see the sea of people and the tools and attitudes they'd brought. Some of these people didn't even know who I was, but when Calla had called and asked them for help, they hadn't stopped to think twice.

Now, with everyone on Owen's front lawn, huddling together and trying to stay as quiet as they could, I approached the door with my bag from Coffeebou and a cat-who-ate-the-canary grin on my face.

Excitement twittered within my chest. And when, after a few seconds of knocking, Owen opened the door, I wedged my foot between the doorjamb and the door, and held the handle with my free hand.

"Good morning, Owen," I chirped.

"Good morning, Virginia." His eyebrows pulled close together in amused confusion. "Is there any particular reason you're holding my door like that?"

Ignoring him, I slipped the Coffeebou bag through the small slit in the door. I had plans for this grand reveal, and I wasn't going to let it get ruined by his question. "I brought coffee. And a bagel. Your usual."

"Thank you. But you still haven't explained the weird door thing."

My cheeks were definitely red now. I could feel the heat in them. Not because I was blushing from embarrassment or anything, but because I was so damned excited I could barely think straight. "It just so happens that I have a surprise for you."

"Oh, yeah? This should be good. What is it?"

"Well…" I turned over my shoulder, flashing a thumbs up to the crowd behind me. "You said that the Engine House needed some TLC, didn't you?"

"Yeah, but the Bride House money—"

I knew exactly what he was going to say next. I knew because it was the reason I came up with this plan. The Fire House needed a new coat of paint and some love both inside and out. Without the money that the town had appropriated to the Bride House, Owen couldn't afford the paint or the labor he needed to make that happen.

But what if he had about fifty free sets of hands to help? And what if someone could convince the town hardware store owner to donate the paint in exchange for Calla not telling his wife about all the times he ignored his doctor's orders to stop ordering donuts from the bakery next door? And what if the local plumber offered to give the internals a thorough inspection and tune-up? And what if an entire class of high schoolers were already in their paint clothes, ready to get their hands dirty and make this place shine?

What if I could get an entire community to come together and give Owen everything he wanted and needed? What if, together, we could make things better?

"The thing is, I called some friends. And they called some friends. And they said as long as they get to play with the puppies for a few minutes…"

That's when I released the door, letting it loose back into Owen's grip and giving him a full view of the yard behind me.

"Then they'd be happy to help you give the old place a facelift."

Behind me, the crowd cheered and shouted out good mornings and hellos, but I kept my eyes firmly on Owen's face. What had been a perplexed expression turned into one of genuine shock and awe.

There might also have been tears in his eyes. But for both of our sakes, I didn't mention it.

He didn't speak. Not at first. And when he did, his voice broke.

"Virginia…"

Instead of letting him finish that thought, I placed a hand on one of his strong shoulders and squeezed. There would be time for emotions and talking later. Right now, we had a fire station to facelift. "They're waiting for you. Tell them what you need."

Owen didn't need to be told twice. Clearing his throat and rubbing his eyes, he marched down and began the work. A spring in his step I'd never quite seen before accompanying him all the way.

Hours and a sandwich break later—courtesy of Coffeebou in town, because Mr. Sanz told me that Owen had bought enough coffee over the years to keep his business booming—the initial furor of the day had somewhat died down. The coats of paint on the house were drying, giving Calla time to direct a group of Willa and her peers in the fine art of flower bed planting. Several of the adults who'd worked through the day were testing the new mechanics of the automatic door they'd fixed in the front of the garage. Several folks were enjoying beers on the grass in front of the house, relaxing in the last of the afternoon sunshine. Inside, I could hear the drilling and hammering of some of the gentlemen who'd volunteered their time today fixing some of the fixtures and dated appliances within.

I sat with the puppies, most of whom were snoozing after a long day of pets and belly rubs and chases through the freshly cut grass.

"I didn't think I'd ever get you alone."

At the sound of Owen's voice, I looked up at his towering figure currently casting a long shadow along my body. He'd changed out of the pajamas in which he'd answered the door, slipping into one of those jeans and T-shirt sets that gave me goosebumps. Slightly too-tight, slightly worn, perfect for me to ogle his perfect body.

"Me?" I scoffed, trying to think about anything but his body and how it would feel under my hands. "You're the popular one today."

Until today, I'd never really thought of Owen as a popular guy. He was the strong and silent type; the kind of man everyone respected, but no one would call their close, personal friend or anything so intimate. But now, I saw that the respect I'd seen from everyone in town was now something deeper: an abiding love for this man, for this member of their community.

I wondered what it would be like, to have that kind of love. To be cared for in such a way. Maybe I would know, one day.

"I'm…" Owen began, reminding me of the last time we'd had one of these important talks of ours. His lips twisted, as if too many words were fighting to get out all at once. "I have so much that I want to say to you, but I don't know where to start."

"Just open your mouth and see what comes out. That's usually how you have conversations like this one."

From the corner of my eye, I watched as some of his ticks of uncertainty came back to him. He cleared his throat too many times. Flexed and clenched his hands. Stared at anything except me.

"When I moved to Fortune Springs, I really cut myself off from people. I'm always friendly, but I'm not really a friend to anyone. I just keep my head down, do my job, and do my best to be nice enough, but not too nice, when people talk to me."

"And…?"

"And I guess… I guess I didn't realize that anyone actually cared about me out here." Before us, the house filled with neighbors and friends and acquaintances seemed larger and closer than it had before, as the man beside me seemed to realize what I already knew. That he was deeply, deeply loved. In spite of his mistakes. In spite of his past. They loved him anyway. "I didn't realize that they would do something like this. I didn't realize that *you* cared about me this much, to set it all up."

I could have told him then and there that the folks tending to the Fire House weren't the only ones who loved him, but I bit down hard on the inside of my lip to keep that revelation from slipping out. Maybe I should keep that one to myself for now.

Besides… if this gesture didn't look like love, if he didn't feel in today everything I felt for him, then I didn't think any words would be enough to convince him.

"This job, protecting these people, it's meant more to me than I can express. And for you to care about it… to do something about it…"

He was struggling with the words, but I knew what he was going to say before he even began. *This means so much to me; thank you for letting it be important to you, too.*

"You don't have to say it. I know."

With that, I slipped my free hand in his. After a moment of hesitation, he answered the gesture, clinging to my hand as if it were the only thing tethering him to the ground. Together, we watched the sunset behind the Fire House. Watched as the paint dried. Watched as the children laughed in the flower beds. Watched as the garage door opened and closed with a mechanical ease.

And as we sat there, watching this old house get rebuilt, I wondered what it would be like to hold his hand for the rest of my life.

Chapter Twenty-One

Days passed as I tried to adjust to this new life I was living. More open. More free. And as honest as I'd ever been in my entire life. And then, one day, I had to go to the mailbox.

I wasn't quite sure how the news had spread to *everyone* I knew and cared about. But somehow, they'd all gotten the memo that I was taking my graduate school application to be mailed, and they'd all invited themselves along.

Willa watched me with excited, careful eyes. "Should we kiss the envelope for good luck?"

"No, dear," Calla replied. "You've got to rub it for good luck. You don't kiss things for good luck, that would be ridiculous."

Willa and Calla flanked my right side, while Owen strode easily along my left like a mismatched angel and devil set sitting on either of my shoulders. Our crew was so extensive it flooded off of the pavement and out onto the grass beyond, but no matter how fast I walked towards the bright blue mailbox down on the corner of State Street and Commerce, I couldn't manage to lose any of them.

"I don't know," Owen said. Without even checking, I could tell from the brassy tone of his voice that he was smirking. Possibly even winking. "I could think of a few things I'd like to kiss for good luck."

Not that I really *wanted* to lose them of course. Maybe they were filling my stomach with butterflies, but even that was better than submitting my grad school application by myself. With them, I might have had nerves, but I also had friends. Support. That meant more to me than anything.

"You're all making me so nervous."

"Oh, I don't want to hear it, young lady," Calla huffed in that half-teasing, half-serious way of hers. The kind that made me feel like just another one of the family. "We shouldn't even be *talking* about luck. You don't need it."

Finally, we made it to my blue haven, the small box at the corner where I would release my hard work from the last few weeks and eventually face my judgment. Some of its edges—which had worn away by time or by distracted, picking hands, I couldn't tell which—revealed their original silver beneath the paint, and those spots glinted maliciously in the sunlight, taunting me. I gripped the heavy manila envelope in my hands. Hopefully no one would notice how tightly I was holding the darn thing.

"Did you really *all* need to walk me the two blocks to this mailbox? It seems a little excessive."

Calla practically crowed, slightly defensive. "Well, I wanted a picture for posterity, but you know I'm useless with a camera phone, so Willa just had to come along."

Owen beamed. "And I had to come along because I'm nosey."

I elbowed him. Jerk. "Hey!"

"And I wanted to support you. Obviously. This is a pretty big moment."

It was, wasn't it? At least, it felt big. Big for me, anyway. After letting someone tell me for so long that I was stupid, that I would never amount to anything on my own, I was now trying. Maybe I would fail. But at least I would try. This time, no one was going to stand in my way.

"Let's just hope we have a *bigger* moment in a few weeks," I muttered. "Something to really celebrate instead of a letdown or a rejection."

Calla didn't let my slight return to realism faze her. "You'll get in, my dear. Don't worry."

"Alright. Here goes nothing."

I went to slip the letter into the mailbox, but the journey was stopped when Calla held out her hand, waving it to stop me. I did, and she turned her attention to her granddaughter.

"Wait! Willa, take the picture!"

Nothing for it. Arguing with Calla at a time like this never ended well, so I posed for the picture with my biggest, cheesiest grin, then waited to finally drop the damn thing until Calla checked her granddaughter's handiwork and nodded that I could continue.

"Perfect. Absolutely perfect. This is going up on the Bride House website."

With one final release of the tight joints in my fingers, I let the envelope slip into the mailbox. I would have thought such a gesture would be more momentous. That maybe a thunderstorm would suddenly swoop in, portending my doom. Or maybe the opposite: that a ray of golden sunshine would descend upon me, blessing me with its rays.

Neither happened. And in the split second that it took to close the mailbox behind me, I realized why. It was because it didn't matter.

Yes, this was something I wanted, badly. But if I got rejected, I wouldn't fall apart. Because now, I had more to live for. With Owen and Willa and Calla at my side, even disappointment and heartbreak would be bearable. Because I had them.

Together, we turned back towards the Bride House, but something stuck in my mind. Something Calla had just said.

"Wait, we have a website?"

"Yes, Doc set it up for me. He's been really helpful lately."

From my right, Owen let out something that sounded suspiciously like a knowing chuckle. "I bet he has."

My eyes widened slightly. Owen didn't usually resort to sultry tones, so the fact that he did so now captured my keenest interest. I snapped my head in Calla's direction. "Who's Doc?"

"No one," she said, just at the same time as Owen said, "The man who's been in love with her for years."

Before my shock at that particular statement could even register on my face, Calla's went slightly red. A dead giveaway that whatever Owen was talking about had hit a nerve. "Owen Harris, this is why I don't speak to you unless it's absolutely necessary! You have absolutely no sense of occasion. We aren't talking about *me*; we're talking about Virginia here."

Willa piped in: "I think we should celebrate with some ice cream. Just an idea."

"Actually, I have a celebration of my own planned. If that's okay, Virginia?"

Owen stopped our merry little caravan now, and when we did, he was all nerves and excitement. I'd never seen him look this way before. Ice cream had sounded appealing, but this… it intrigued me.

"Really?"

"Yeah. It's a small thing. Nothing to really think too much about."

"Are you sure?"

"Yeah."

I glanced at Calla, who gave me the smallest of nods. With her confidence, I allowed myself to accept what I wanted: more time alone with Owen.

"Well, girls, I'll see you back at the house tonight."

Calla winked and led her granddaughter away from us. "I made pork chops. Don't be late or Willa will eat them all before you get there!"

Ten minutes later, he'd taken me on an unfamiliar route through town, passing houses and buildings I'd seen a dozen times before, only in a different order than I'd ever witnessed them previously. I wouldn't have minded, of course, except the promise of a celebration of his own, as he put it, had every neuron in my body firing excited heat. My skin tingled at the thought of whatever it was he had planned right now.

In the past, I would have been afraid of something so unknown like this. But today, I could barely walk in a straight line because I was so excited. The possibilities were endless.

"So," I finally asked, "where *are* we going?"

"Just a little place I know. But the place isn't the surprise. There's something *there* that's the surprise."

He pointed a few paces ahead of us, towards a tall fence I didn't recognize. As we moved closer and closer, I realized that the fence wasn't a fence at all. It was a gate, and at the center of it stood a tall entranceway, framed by metalwork letters emblazoned with the words THE MOUNTAINTOP SCRAPYARD. I'm not sure any other place on Earth he could have chosen would have surprised me more.

It was a humble place, the kind that Stephen King might have written about in one of his more folksy books about growing up in a small town. Scrapyard was a bit of an overstatement, and a delicate one at that. In reality, it was more like a colorful graveyard, where rusted-out car bodies and old hand-cranked washing machines got buried in a sea of discarded hubcaps and metal dress forms. Small sprigs of grass grew out of the dirt beneath the trash, giving the entire place a kind of haunted beauty.

Of all the spots he could have taken me, this was the one I hadn't prepared for. On the walk over here, I'd thought of how I would act if he took me out for pasta or up the mountain on a hike or to the library, or, or, or…

But a junkyard? Even in my wildest imaginings, I hadn't dreamed of a place like this.

"Oh, I'm intrigued."

"Now, close your eyes."

My fight or flight mode flared up. Did I really trust myself—did I really trust this guy—to let down my defenses so heavily in his presence?

Yes. Yes, I did. And just as quickly as the sensation flared up, it disappeared, and my eyes slipped closed.

"Okay."

The air shifted around us as his fingers came to rest on either of my shoulders, guiding me forward. The anticipation built like a storm in the pit of my stomach, swirling and growing until I couldn't help it anymore. I opened one of my eyes, just in time for him to catch my reflection in a shattered mirror propped up against a discarded porcelain bathtub.

"Hey!" he protested, his voice touched with laughter. "No peeking."

"Fine."

"Here. Let me help you, you sneak." This time, when his hands returned to my body, they didn't go to my shoulders, but rather to my face, where he placed his fingers over my eyes, ensuring that I couldn't peek even if I wanted to. "Now, walk forward."

"Okay…"

It was strange, trusting someone this much, but still, when he moved forward, so did I. Together, we walked through a twisting maze of steps—at least, that's how it seemed to me, given my sense of direction was a little skewed given my lack of sight—as the scents of earth and rusted metal filled my lungs with every breath. Eventually, we slowed, then stopped so Owen could adjust my stance to his specifications. *Okay, let's move one step to your left. Mm-hm, and now take about a half step forward. And turn your face a little to the right…*

"And… open."

His hands moved away from my face, and at his direction, I opened my eyes at long last. And while this visit to the junkyard in and of itself had been a surprise, what greeted me when I finally blinked the sun from my eyes… nothing could have prepared me for it.

There, only a few feet away, was a van. Painted a deep, soothing blue, its great body was broken up by intricately painted white signage done in an old-school 70s style that would have looked just as at home on the cover of a Heart album. Its swirling white letters read: VIRGINIA BESSEL ANIMAL THERAPY – FOR WHEN TIMES GET RUFF.

Even with the cheesy slogan, even with the slightly wonky front left tire, even with the small rusting spots wearing away some of the van's corners, it was perfect. After a moment of staring at it, I had to remind myself to breathe. It was *literally* breathtaking.

"What is this?"

Owen's excited steps moved from behind me, and he practically bounded towards the van, placing his hands on it like he was the over-caffeinated host of one of those renovation shows Calla watched compulsively. "Now, I know it's a little bit early, and I don't want to jinx anything. But my buddy was selling this, and I thought… hey, Virginia's going to need a van when she starts her business, so… I got him to donate it."

"It's… It's a van. For my business."

I was stating the obvious now, but the implications of this gesture, the weight and force of it, was making rational thought almost impossible. It wasn't *just* a slightly crappy van tucked away in the depths of a junkyard. It was a statement of belief. He *believed* in me. He believed in my dream enough to tell someone else about it, ask them for their van, and repaint it with the name of a business I hadn't even started yet. One I wasn't even yet qualified for.

I'd never had anyone believe in me this way. Never had someone see this much in me. Never had anyone look forward to my future and seen something beautiful there. How did you thank someone for giving you a gift that precious? How did you put into words how special a revelation like that was?

The truth was, you didn't. And I couldn't.

My silence, though, didn't sit well with Owen. From the corner of my eye—which was still locked on the van and all of its less than pristine glory—I noticed his face fall. His skin went pale and lifeless, then tinged with pink embarrassment.

"You hate it."

"No," I said, my voice breaking on even that simple word. "It's the most beautiful thing I've ever seen. I just don't know what to say."

"Say you'll take me for a drive in it?"

Joy returned to him; a conspiratorial grin illuminated his face. Opening the front door with a flourish, he opened it up to me, gesturing that I should go inside. I stepped towards him to answer the gesture and take a look inside.

My knowledge of vans wasn't what anyone would call extensive, but from what I'd seen in movies and television, this looked no better or worse than a van like this was supposed to look. Slightly worn and cracked tan leather seats and bench-rows. Carpet that had been so thoroughly cleaned over the years that it slightly matted in some places. A kitschy lumberjack talisman behind the rearview mirror.

But there was one thing that gave me pause. One thing above everything else that dragged a cloud across my currently sunshine-drenched disposition.

"Well, I would, but there's only one problem."

Worry flashed in his eyes as they met mine. "Yeah?"

"I don't know how to drive a stick."

Chapter Twenty-Two

At my revelation, Owen's chin dropped in the sexiest look of surprise I'd ever seen a man flash. I don't know if it was the dizzying high of getting such a thoughtful, personal gift or the fact that he was so close to me now, but either way, I was stunned by it.

"So, you've never driven one of these?"

"A giant van with my name painted on the side?" I teased. "No, I can't say I have."

"I meant a stick, smart aleck."

"Nope, not even once."

Truth be told, I didn't do a whole lot of my own driving in general. I knew how to drive an automatic and had gotten my license when I turned sixteen like everyone else, but all my life, I hadn't owned my own car. Porter had done the driving for the both of us in my last relationship—all the better to keep me on a short leash. Not having a car of my own meant I depended on him every time I wanted to go into town or see anyone or do anything. It made my world small.

But if I could learn how to drive this van, then I wouldn't just have my freedom, I would have a career, too. Opportunity. Possibility.

Leaning up against the front door, which was still propped open, Owen raised a charming eyebrow up at me, poking and prodding me with his abrupt, friendly gaze.

"Aren't you from the country? I thought all country girls knew how to do things like this better than guys do."

My lips tugged even further upward, something I hadn't even known was possible given the fact that I was already beaming. "Is it still a sexist assumption if it's complimentary?"

"Alright, alright. I'm sorry. Here. Let's get in. I'll show you how to drive this beauty."

Beauty was not what I would have called it. It was beautiful for what it represented, not for its actual looks. The van, as they said, had a good personality. It was clearly an older model—the tape deck in the center of the dashboard told me that it was even older than I'd originally suspected—and when I pulled myself into the driver's seat, I realized that there was *only* a driver's seat. Like many older models, this one didn't have two separate seats for the driver and front passenger, but one aging, leather bench for both of us.

Without my permission, my mind flashed to what *other* things this bench seat would be good for. My mind conjured images of Owen's hands wandering, my body giving, the windows fogging.

Slam. The heavy thud of the passenger door snapped me out of that particular daydream, thankfully, and I put my hands on ten and two, ready for my first stick lesson.

Thankfully, this part of the junkyard was clear of any pedestrians. If I hit anything, it would just be one of the other junker cars out here in the scrap metal graveyard.

For a moment, I didn't do anything. I just sat behind the wheel, holding it and looking out of the window, imagining what it would be like, driving this van into my future. I knew it was probably a small thing to anyone else—plenty of grown women in America drove their own cars every single day—but to me, it was everything. It was freedom. It was the key to the open road and a future of my own making and my own design.

Driving this therapy-mobile would help me claim my own destiny, and that… that meant everything. I could feel my own excitement run through me, an engine powering every inch of my body as my hands shook from the sheer force of it.

"Hey, Virginia?" Owen asked after a long moment.

"Yeah?"

"You need to put the key into the ignition first. Same as a regular car."

Damn. Right. I wasn't the only person in the car. Scrambling for the keys—which were tucked up in the sun visor over the driver's seat—I laughed at myself in the most self-deprecating way possible.

"I was getting to that." I scraped my mind for some kind of lie. "I was just… connecting with the car."

"Yeah, and what does that entail?"

This time, it wasn't so much of a lie as it was a joke. "Well, she's got to have a name. All good vans have one, or so I'm told."

"And you communicate telepathically with the van to find that name out, do you?"

Checking my mirrors—the only thing I knew how to do in a car like this—I swallowed the urge to pull him closer and forget about the driving lesson altogether.

"You're impossible. Just tell me how to drive this thing."

"You're going to want to start by pressing down on the clutch pedal. It'll either have a stopping point, or it'll just go until it touches the floor. Every car is different, so you'll need to feel it out."

After accidentally touching the brake *and* the accelerator before finally just asking him which one was the "clutch" pedal, I managed to do the bare minimum. "Done."

"Now, keep that down, and while you're doing that—"

"Wouldn't it just be easier to call an Uber any time I want to bring the puppies to a therapy session?"

He barked a laugh, and the sound, combined with the teasing scolding he gave me next, brought him even closer to me.

"Do you want to learn to drive this thing or not?"

I was breathless again, and it had everything to do with him. "Sorry, teach."

In this enclosed space, it was impossible to get away from him, even if I wanted to, which I didn't. His big, muscular body seemed to be everywhere. His warmth permeated the still air. Even his scent filled my nose, leaving me slightly dizzy. I was completely overwhelmed by him—not just by the beauty of him and the nearness of him, but by my own feelings for him.

Then, he had to go and make it worse.

"Now—Do you mind if I touch you?"

"No," I said.

The moment I spoke, I knew I'd said that entirely too fast and too eager. But there was no taking it back now. With deliberate care, he closed most of the gap between us on the bench seat, and the desire I had to close what little space there was left was nearly enough to set me ablaze. Lacing his fingers through mine, he drew my right hand to the gear stick.

Goosebumps awakened along my skin. I was holding my breath. There was no way he couldn't tell. My mind and my body were torn, one distracted by the task at hand and the other distracted by him.

"Okay, you're just going to put your hand here, and I'll help you put it—"

We pressed down on the stick together, and dragged the car into first. My skin flushed with his breath against my collarbone. "Wait, I don't think I'm doing this—"

"Now, press down on the accelerator. Gently now." I did as he instructed, and the car spurred forward. "You're doing great. You're moving."

I'm moving. I'm moving. And Owen Harris is beside me. He's touching me. Without thinking about the ramifications, I turned to face him so I could crow about my accomplishments.

"I did it! I'm moving!"

"Wait, don't crash—"

Right! Crashing. I didn't want to do that. Wrenching my hand away from his, I yanked on the emergency brake, drawing us to a sharp stop just before we ran into a pile of junk straight ahead of us.

Certainly not the most spectacular almost-crash anyone had ever been involved with. But my adrenaline kicked in all the same.

"Sorry," I breathed.

He chuckled. "It's alright. I actually *did* crash my first time driving a stick. And that was an actual fire truck, so…"

"What?"

"Yeah, you should really see the look on a cop's face when they come to the sight of a crash into a light pole and see that it was a fire truck that did it. So, there. You're already doing better than me and you've only gone, what? Five feet."

We were staring at each other now. Incredibly close. Closer than we'd ever been before. I was dizzy with him, with the wanting of him. The words tumbled out of me before I could manage to stop them.

Not that I would have wanted to stop them. Not if I'd known what would come next.

"Hey, Owen?"

"Yeah?"

He glanced at my lips. It wasn't my imagination. He wanted me, too.

"You know what they say about adrenaline? How it makes you want to do crazy things?"

"I've heard that," he agreed.

"Is it true? I'm guessing you're the expert."

He took my hand again. Soft. Yearning.

"It's true. But if you're talking about this... about us... about what I want to do right now... then I don't think it's the adrenaline."

I didn't know what to think about that—heartbroken or hopeful. I glanced up at him from under my dark eyelashes.

"Really?"

"Really. Because I've been wanting to do this for a really, really long time."

It was as if we were one person, moving with one thought and one desire. As soon as those words were past his lips, they collided into mine, breathing new life into my broken chest and filling it with all the love, all the desire, all the acceptance I'd ever wanted.

My first lesson in driving a stick shift didn't much progress past that point. Every time we broke apart for air and tried to return to the task at hand, we found ourselves distracted yet again by the pull of our lips. The closeness of our bodies in the truck cab. The fire smoldering between us.

But, eventually, we had to return home. The walk was slower getting away from the junkyard as it had been walking to it, but that's only because we took every shadow and every secluded nook and cranny on the way as an invitation to capture "one last" kiss before we parted.

By the time we reached the Bride House, the sun had settled behind the horizon and the path through the streets of town became illuminated by starlight and lightning bugs and lamplight. The night was cool and clear and crisp and the moonlight spilled over us, as if the entire universe had conspired to give this evening the fairy tale ending it deserved.

The lights in the house were completely extinguished, telling me that either I'd missed pork chop night or Calla and Willa had realized I wouldn't be home in time and gone out to eat something else so we could share dinner another night. Either way, I was sure I was in for an earful when I saw Calla again, but this time, I didn't care.

Owen and I parted at the gate, and with every step back towards home, I realized something. This was the start. I was standing on the brink of something great and wonderful, and finally, no one—not myself, not anyone from my past, not my fears or doubts or struggles—were going to stand in my way. With my lips still tingling and slightly swollen from Owen's kisses, my entire body hummed in expectation. What would tomorrow bring? What new adventures would I face then? How would the world feel now that I'd decided to face it, head-on?

But those questions went unanswered. New ones took their place. Because when I opened my bedroom door, the lamplight flickered on… revealing a figure in the corner. A familiar figure with a familiar voice that sent a familiar chill up and down my spine.

"Hello, Virginia."

Chapter Twenty-Three

It was as if someone had slipped an ice cube down the back of my shirt. Cold trickled down my spine. I froze. My heart stopped. The wires in my mind short-circuited, frying all of my capacity to think and feel properly. The only two words that came to mind repeated over and over again, on a loop, like some kind of twisted merry-go-round tune.

He's here. He's here. He's here.

I opened my mouth to call Calla. To call Willa. To call anyone. But the man in the window just smiled.

"You'd be wasting your breath."

Without moving my head, I scanned the darkness until I found his form sitting in my chair in the corner, submerged in shadow. Even from this distance, I could see the swell of his massive shoulders and scent the stale tang of cigarette smoke in the air all around him. He'd found me.

"Your two friends went to the movies in the next county over. Won't be back for hours. You know, it's amazing what you overhear in a small-town diner. They were going to see some flick and go for ice cream after. The town librarian is hooking up with the fry cook. And you… you were out somewhere in the mountains with a man."

"How did you—"

"How did I find you?" He stood up. I flinched to move backwards and retreat, but the rest of my muscles refused to obey. When he continued speaking, I could barely hear him over the hammering of my heart. "Was a damned tricky thing, you know. Had to pull all kinds of favors. But you really should have known better than to plan your little escape on our house's Wi-Fi."

That's when he stepped from the shadows into the small expanse of light afforded by the room's only lamp, and I saw him in fullness for the first time. My stomach—no, my entire being—revolted at the sight of him. Porter had always been obsessed with appearances. Never left the house without his hair done. Never let me go out in public in tennis shoes or anything close to casual wear. He didn't know how to disappoint, at least visually. His community was known to exile anyone who left even the slightest wrinkle unattended.

But that was not the Porter standing in front of me. His rumpled T-shirt might once have been a pristine white, but today, it was almost yellowed from unidentifiable stains. His mussed hair hung loose over his eyes, and those eyes were bleary and unfocused. Tired. Smoke-shot. At least three days of stubble collected on his chin; he'd tossed his contacts for thick, black glasses that did nothing to hide the deep bags beneath his eyes and the puffy swollen mounds of his cheeks.

Him showing up out of nowhere had been frightening enough. But for him to show up looking like this? An icy stab pierced my heart. He'd never been entirely stable before. This was proof that he'd completely severed any last ties he might have had to his control.

"What happened, V? Was I really so bad to you?"

"Please don't call me that."

My voice was barely more than a whisper, but I couldn't let him get away with the nickname, no matter how weak the protestation came out. I'd hated the nickname back when we'd been together, and I despised it now, especially when he delivered it on a cloud of nicotine-tainted breath.

Especially now, when I knew how sweet it felt to hear your name spoken by someone who actually cared about you.

"You *have* changed," he snorted. "You used to love it when I called you that."

Porter circled me. I stayed rooted to the floor. There wasn't going to be any escaping this. The second-floor window was too high to jump from and I knew I'd never outrun him if I went for the door. I fought for control of my voice, of myself, as I responded.

"No, I didn't. Every time I told you I didn't, you laughed me off and said it was your special nickname for me, so it didn't matter what I thought."

Oh, V. Don't be so modest. Every guy's best girl needs a cute little nickname. It could be worse. I could use a different v-word to describe you, couldn't I?

"I can see the distance hasn't done anything for your attitude," he muttered.

That's when the circling stopped. Facing me head-on, he was in the perfect spot to start charging me, and that's exactly what he did. Not like a brutish animal, but like a hunter, carefully backing his prey into a corner. At first, I tried to resist, tried to hold my ground, but it was no use. Soon, I was matching him step for step, working my way back into the wall behind me.

"Why are you here?"

"Would you believe it if I said I'd missed you?"

"Yes."

My spine pressed into the wallpaper. Nowhere to run. The cage of his body trapped me. Of course he would miss me. I'd done everything for him. Washed his clothes and polished his floors and driven him home when he'd gotten "gentleman drunk" at one of his family's parties.

As he got even closer to me, the scent of that same liquor—aged whiskey—brushed against my face. I swallowed back the river of bile threatening the back of my throat.

"Well, I missed you. And I think it's right about time you come home."

"But—"

"I know every woman is entitled to have a little fun," he said, as though *he* was the rational one and I was the one making no sense. "A little time off the leash. I don't blame you, V. But we've had enough of this now, and it's time for you to come home. Where you belong. Come on, pack up your things."

"I'm supposed to stay here for a year. It's a whole agreement. I can't just leave."

Just say no. It's not hard. It's one of the smallest words in the English language and the easiest to pronounce. Just say it.

But the truth was, I knew how much power it took to say a word like *no*. Against someone like Porter, it was an almost impossible word to use, like a witch's curse that demanded blood from whomever so much as uttered it. Excuses, I could do. Outright refusing him? I knew the consequences of trying something like that, and I wasn't ready to face them. I didn't know how.

He smiled. It was clear he thought of the matter as settled. Turning on his heel, he started rummaging through my things. "I'm sure they'll understand. Where's your bag?"

"It's up in the attic," I lied. "Somewhere up there and I couldn't possibly—"

Before I could finish the thought, he found my backpack's hiding place beneath the bed. He held it up triumphantly.

"You were saying?"

All at once, I realized that this was one of those Moments. One of those Moments where I could choose to be brave. Where I could choose to fight despite the odds stacking up higher and higher against me. If I didn't start now, I knew I was going to be lost forever. Squaring my shoulders, I gathered up all my courage. "I was saying no. No. I'm not going with you. I'm staying here."

He paused. "I don't understand."

From experience, I knew that a comment like that was more of a warning than a real expression of confusion. But the fire beneath my skin had already ignited, and I could no longer control it. I may have left him in the night to avoid this kind of confrontation, but now that I'd started, I couldn't hold back the years of pent-up feelings now exploding out of me. "I'm staying here in Fortune Springs. You know, I thought that running halfway across the country and leaving no forwarding address would have been enough to get through your thick skull. We're broken up. Done. I've left you. We're through. And that means I don't have to go anywhere with you. Ever again."

My voice raised at the end, almost to a scream, and that seemed to be what clinched it. Something shifted in Porter's eyes as he realized I wasn't going to back down as easily as I used to. I was going to fight him on this, not just follow where he led.

In that instant, I knew I was in more danger than ever before. Now, I'd broken his last hope. Now, he had nothing left to lose.

"We aren't through," he said, his voice a low warning.

"Yes. We are. I'm staying in Fortune Springs and you need to leave. I'm happy here. Happier than I ever was with you."

He was approaching now. A wounded hunter. More dangerous. Less predictable.

"If you keep talking you're going to say something you can't take back."

"I don't want to take any of it back. Not when I'm finally telling the truth."

"I see. So, this is about your sweetheart? The firefighter?"

A minute ago, I'd felt like I was winning. At least like I was free. Telling the truth at long last. But the moment he stopped at the floorboards in front of me and said those words, *the firefighter*, I knew that I hadn't even been playing the same game as Porter, much less winning it. The confidence returned to his eyes as my voice shook.

"How do you know about him?"

"Told you. Word travels fast at a small-town diner. Sit there with a cup of coffee long enough and you'll learn everything you ever need to know."

The danger lurking in Porter's hulking body rattled me to the core, but I tried to remain strong. To divert the man's attention away from Owen and back onto me.

"This doesn't have anything to do with him. This is about us. About me."

"Right. About you wanting to trade me in for someone else."

"I didn't come here looking for him, but I did come here looking to get *away* from you."

I might as well have slapped him. But he didn't reel back like I wanted him to. Instead, he raised a hand to my cheek, his touch more firm and direct than tender and caring.

"And why is that? What did I ever do to you but love you and look after you and want you to be a better person? I took you out of the trailer-trash gutter where you came from and made you into a woman. How ungrateful can you be?"

"I just want a life of my own."

A tear trickled down my cheek. I couldn't help it. And I hated myself for that. But with every possible feeling fighting inside of me for attention—rage, hurt, fear, pride—trying to fight the tears was just too much to ask.

"And you're getting a life of your own by shacking up with some nobody firefighter?"

"Who is more of a man than you'll ever be."

The words were out of my mouth before I could stop them. And I didn't regret them. Not at first. Not until a meaty paw of a hand slammed against my neck, sending my skull flying into the wall behind me and my windpipe buckling beneath Porter's palm. He was on me then, too close.

"Okay, now, listen to me and listen good. I did not invest all of this time and money and care into you for you to just throw it away. Do you know how it's been for me, having to face everyone back home without you at my side? The kinds of questions I've been forced to answer? The kinds of gossip that I've been subjected to?"

"I—"

"Shut up."

I did, and immediately. Not because I was so used to taking his orders that it came naturally to me, but because his grip on my windpipe tightened considerably when he spoke. This was the violence I'd run away to escape. The cruel, casual brutality that was slowly wrapping its way around his heart and controlling everything he did.

"I want us to be happy. Don't you want to be happy?"

When I didn't answer right away, he loosened the grip on my neck just long enough for me to nod once. In my playbook against this man, I only had a few courses open to me. One of them? Placation until escape was possible. That's all I could do right now. Play along until I could get myself free. I'd done it before, hadn't I? I could do it again.

"Then you need to come home with me. I would hate for anything to happen to this little town because of you. Or to your firefighter."

My heart stopped again. Firefighter. The town. The veiled—thinly, thinly veiled—threat. Moving his hand from my throat to my cheek, he cupped me uncomfortably, not so much beholding me as holding me in place.

"What do you mean?"

"I mean it's time for you to come home. And if that means making sure you don't have any reason to stay here, I will absolutely do it."

His voice lowered, and the threat became real. No, not a threat. A promise. After all the time I'd spent gathering up my courage, it all drained out of me in an instant. I could not let any harm come to anyone in Fortune Springs. Not because of me. Not when I could prevent it.

"Okay. Okay," I breathed, forcing a weak, shaky smile. "We don't need to rush into anything."

"I'm not rushing. I'm just telling you how it is. God, I've missed you so much, V."

With that, he crumbled into me, dragging me into his arms. He wrapped me in a hug, blissfully giving me time to let my face do some crumbling of its own.

"I'll need some time," I breathed, trying not to gag at the smell of his cigarette-stained shirt. "To pack. To say my goodbyes."

When he pulled away, he held me at arm's-length, sizing me up. I did my best to look honest. Honestly excited about a future with him. I wasn't sure he bought it, but he started moving towards the bedroom door, apparently more confident in the power of his threats than my devotion to him.

"I'll wait downstairs. Pack up, and I'll drive you where you need to go. And remember what I said, won't you?"

"I will."

By some miracle, I was able to hold back my sobs until I heard him reach the first floor of the house.

Chapter Twenty-Four

I shoved everything in my bag in a rush of fabric and limbs. My one and only goal right now was to get out of the house as fast as I could. To get away before Calla came home and found me. I didn't think I could face her.

The other thing I wasn't sure I could face? What I had to do next.

Taking out sheets of paper from the notebook I'd written drafts of my college entrance essay in, I scribbled down a handful of words in a rush. Thoughts and feelings poured out of me, but I stopped them before the pen could capture any of them.

We both needed a clean break. Owen deserved that.

I also left a note for Calla and Willa. Much shorter. Somehow, I felt that the longer the letter was, the more disappointed in me Calla would have been. And I couldn't stand the thought of her disappointment.

Once I'd left the letter on my dresser, I shouldered my backpack and headed downstairs. We needed to be fast. To get out before anyone saw my failure. Thankfully, Porter seemed equally eager to get out of town. After ushering me into the front seat, he allowed me to point him to a small corner a stretch away from the Fire

House, where I slipped from his truck and into the shadows that led me straight to Owen's place.

And to Owen himself, who wasn't, as I'd hoped, deeply asleep with our little puppies, and was instead sitting on his porch swing, flipping through a book. I froze at the top of the porch when his eyes pierced mine through the darkness.

"Oh," I said, dropping my eyes to the floorboards at my feet. "I didn't think you'd still be awake."

He chuckled, but an unseen tension choked the sound. "Why'd you come over here if you didn't want me to be awake?"

Instead of responding, I only shrugged. I was sure that, by now, I looked like a human collection of red flags, but Owen chose to ignore them. I didn't blame him. After all, we'd had the most amazing day together. The kiss was still fresh in my mind, so surely it was still fresh in his. It only made sense that he'd ignore any negative, weird vibes I was putting off in favor of pretending everything was as okay as it had been this afternoon.

"The pups were keeping me awake. I wanted to make sure they all got to sleep okay before I went to sleep myself. Hey, I'm sorry, why don't you come in? I'll get you a cup of coffee and we can—"

"No," I said, too fast and too harsh to be natural. Owen's face shifted, but I pretended as though I didn't see it.

"It's alright, really. I'm not even a little bit tired. We can sit out here and talk if you want. Or if coffee isn't what you're in the mood for—"

"I didn't come here for coffee or anything else. I didn't come here to talk to you. I just…"

Almost unconsciously, my hand tightened around the letter in my fist. I could feel his eyes travel down to it.

"Are you alright? Don't take this the wrong way, but you don't look very well."

"I'm having a bad night is all. I'm exhausted."

"Then you definitely need that cup of coffee," he said, his tone begging me to laugh. To smile. To do anything but stare at the damn floorboards and ignore him.

He should have been more careful what he wished for. Because I did something different. I turned my blazing eyes on him and practically hissed my reply.

"I didn't come here for coffee, dammit! I came here to tell you that I'm leaving."

He didn't speak for a long moment. The color drained from his face.

"You're what?"

"I'm leaving. I have to go."

Once again, I returned to not looking at him. Surely, that would make this easier. Maybe he would let me go faster. The last thing I wanted was for Porter to come over here and ruin everything. I needed to leave, and fast.

"Like… away for the weekend?"

"Don't be stupid. I'm *going*, okay? For good."

I fought to keep my voice steady. Cold. Detached. It was the most difficult thing I'd ever done.

"I don't understand," he said.

"There isn't anything for you to understand."

"But today… everything that's been happening between us. I thought you finally trusted me."

"I—"

"And what about the Bride House? What about Calla and Willa?"

"They'll be better off."

That was the one thing in this whole thing that I knew to be true. I'd been nothing but trouble from the moment I arrived in Fortune Springs. Maybe my leaving would bring everyone a little bit of peace.

I couldn't give them much, but at least I could give them that.

Owen's voice broke when he spoke again. "What changed?"

"Nothing. Everything. I don't know. I just… Take this. It'll explain."

It wouldn't, but telling the truth had stopped mattering to me, really. I just needed to get out of here safely. To get Porter far away from anyone I cared about.

"But you're here. I'm here. Why wouldn't you just explain to me now? What is wrong?"

"What's wrong is that I can't stay here. I'm not the kind of person who gets a life like this, okay? That's just how it is and how it has to be."

The ends of my sentences were jagged and raw, the sound of someone who'd been crying all night, but I didn't let a single tear slip down my cheek.

"The kind of person you are is whoever you want to be. Nothing is set in stone. Don't run away from something good just because you don't think you deserve it."

"I'm leaving now. I have to."

That was the line in the sand. I was going. End of story. When I looked up at him one last time, I could see that everything in him wanted to cross that line. To hold me close and beg me to stay and whisper love and encouragement and hope into my ear. But he couldn't be that man. I'd spent so much of my life being ordered around by others. Being controlled by others. He wouldn't do it, too. Not even if losing me meant breaking his own heart.

That's just the kind of man he was. Good. Even when it cost him everything.

"Well. I can't stop you. But… you should know—"

I knew what he was going to say before he said it. But the thought of living with those words and their memory forever in my heart was too painful to bear. I held up one hand and snapped my eyes shut.

"Please. Don't. I don't want to hear it." I shoved the sealed envelope into his hands. "Just take this. Goodbye."

And with that, I turned on my heel and practically flew down the front steps, leaving him alone with his thoughts and my words.

As I left, heading down the street to the place where I'd left Porter in his truck, the words from my own letter flowed through my mind.

Dear Owen,

I never thought I was capable of real love. But I found it with you. The trouble with life is that we can't ever be allowed to keep the things that mean the most to us. Please, look after the pups and tell everyone I'm sorry. But Fortune Springs... I just don't belong here.

Virginia.

Thoughts of the letter leadened my steps, but I carried on anyway. Down the street. And into the cab of the truck, where I closed the door behind me with a heavy, solid, final *thud*.

"So," Porter asked. "Who was that?"

"No one."

But I knew—we both knew—that that wasn't true at all.

Porter hit the gas so hard the tires squealed as we headed straight out of Fortune Springs.

Chapter Twenty-Five

The pavement disappeared beneath us, and I let the streets flow past me with my eyes closed. I knew the second I opened them fully, the tears would start falling.

I couldn't afford to cry. Not here. Not now. I needed to be strong.

The truth of it was, I *did* love everyone in Fortune Springs. Owen was right. When I thought of my future now, I didn't see the puppies and the van. I didn't see the acceptance letter with my name on it, arriving at Calla's place. I didn't see long afternoons in the sun with Calla and her granddaughter. I didn't see the happiness I'd once fought so hard for. Instead, I foresaw long days of hunger and longing, of staring out into the distance and aching to come back here. Back to my friends. Back to this town. Back to Owen.

But it was *because* I loved them all that I was willing to make this sacrifice. That I was willing to walk back into the arms of a man who would tighten his grip with every passing day. Because I knew enough about him now to know that there was no limit to his cruelty. He would hurt the people I loved. He would destroy this town. He would break Owen.

And I couldn't allow that to happen. I would rather spend the rest of my miserable life holding on to these memories than allow anyone to hurt the people who had given me so much. It wasn't a trade-off I loved. It would haunt me for the rest of my life. But I knew I was doing the right thing. What was the life of one woman when stacked against the happiness and lives of all the people she loved?

Nothing.

Eventually, I found the strength to open my eyes.

Just in time to see headlights swimming in our vision, and to feel Porter slam painfully on the brakes.

"What's happening?" I breathed.

"Some old lady's stopped in the middle of the road. Don't worry. I'll make sure she moves."

In that moment, two things stuck in the forefront of my mind. One: of course Porter would try to move an old lady instead of help her if she had car trouble. And two: there was only one old lady who could be out here, in the middle of the road at this time of night. I didn't know how I knew. But when Calla appeared at my car window before Porter could even slip out of the driver's seat, not a single part of me was surprised.

"Virginia!"

Every muscle in my body tensed. This was the one person I didn't want to see. The one person I knew I couldn't lie to. The one person who might be able to convince me to stay.

"Calla! What are you... what are you doing here?"

I glanced sidelong to Porter, whose hands tightened around the steering wheel. I knew we didn't have much time for this unwelcome interruption before he blew up over it. Slightly out of breath, Calla clutched the canvas tote slung over her shoulder. A little bit rumpled, but kind, warm, and peak busybody. I could see the cracks in her facade, though. The way she gripped her shoulder bag a little too tightly and the wrinkles at the corners of her eyes showing the effort it took her to keep her smile on.

"Well, we left the movie early because it was too scary for Willa, but then when I got home, I saw some note about you leaving and I knew you wouldn't do that without saying goodbye."

"She's coming back home with me," Porter said, his voice walking a fine line between promise and threat.

"Oh, I realize that. It was in the note, Slick. Don't worry. I haven't come to lure her back home to the house. Just to give her this."

Reaching into her tote, Calla pulled out a small, tin lunchbox and handed it over. Porter, apparently uninterested in this conversation or the lunchbox, took the liberty of fiddling with the radio, filling the background with the static between stations. Apparently, he was all too confident that nothing could change the outcome of this night. I wasn't so sure.

I ran my hands over the small, metal box, which glinted in the lights from the cars with a kind of pretty shine that almost made me sick.

"What is this?" I asked, making no move to open it.

"It's a long drive back to Savannah, isn't it? I thought you could use some little snacks and treats to keep you going along the way."

So, she wasn't going to try and get me to stay? Wasn't going to give me the third degree about running off without an explanation?

Before I could help myself, I reached out of the window and took Calla's soft, worn hands. I knew that where I was going, there weren't any women like Calla. And that thought finally brought tears to my eyes.

"Thank you, Calla."

"And thank you, Virginia," Calla whispered, her voice strong and certain. "You sure weren't with us long, but we were mighty happy to have you."

Beside me, Porter cleared his throat. "Virginia, we've got to get going."

I didn't have the strength to look at Calla any longer. Goodbyes had never been my strong suit. Especially not goodbyes with someone who actually gave a damn about me.

"Well, goodbye."

"Bye, dear."

And just like that, Calla backed away, got in her car, and drove out of the center of the road so Porter could drive on past her, allowing me to turn my back on life here in Fortune Springs. Tucking myself and my lunchbox deeper into the front seat, I stared out into the darkness of the mountain ahead and began the process of mentally cutting myself off from this chapter of my life.

You're doing this to protect them, I reminded myself. *You're doing this to help them.*

Eventually, I forced my eyes away from the road, choosing instead to stare down at the lunchbox in my lap. My last connection to the Bride House, to Calla, to Willa and this time in my life. Carefully, I opened the lid, and began picking through the pieces contained within.

A wrapped peanut butter and jelly sandwich—crusts cut off, of course—, homemade cookies—sugar, cut into the shape of a heart, pink icing—pretzels, a cinnamon bun...

"So," Porter muttered, glancing at the lunchbox. "She's the reason you've gotten so fat lately, huh? Don't worry. We'll get you back to healthy once we get back home. Make sure to dump all that crap at the next rest stop, okay? Don't want it to be tempting you, do we?"

… And a small slip of paper, hidden beneath it all. I stared at it as I spoke, knowing even as my attention narrowed that ignoring him or disagreeing with him wouldn't work in my favor.

"No. Of course not."

The sheet of paper was small. A hidden secret just for me. And in thin, curving, handwriting, a few words blared out from the page. *You can always come home, my dear.*

The mountain road leading out of town loomed large in my vision, and the winding path made me dizzy. I knew, in that moment, that if I let this car get to the other side of this mountain, I'd never come back to Fortune Springs. I'd never be free.

"Could you please pull over?" I said, my breath coming out in quick pants. A plan materialized in my mind. Not much of a plan, mind you, but all I could come up with on a moments' notice. Desperation was driving me now, not logic.

"What?"

"I'm sorry. I'm feeling kind of sick. The winding roads, and everything, you know."

Porter wasn't going to give up his quick getaway quite so easily, though.

"You've got to be kidding me. Can't you wait until the next rest stop?"

Willing my face to turn green, I laid on thick the act of a sick passenger. "No. I don't think I can. I need to get out."

"V—"

I reached for the door handle, implicitly threatening to toss myself out of the moving car if he didn't comply with my will.

"Now."

"Fine. Fine. Don't do anything crazy, now. Just hold it in a second."

In a moment, he pulled off onto the shoulder, near a dense patch of woods. Practically jumping out of the car, I didn't need to look back to confirm that he'd gotten out, too. The guy was useless without his cigarette every fifteen minutes. It was time for him to light up, and my vomiting in the woods wasn't going to get in the way of that.

Pointing towards the thicket, I called over to him. "I'm just going to—"

"Yeah, I don't need to hear it."

Good. Finally, his lack of interest in me was paying off. At first, I kept my walk firm and direct, the kind of walk I imagined people did when they were trying to find a safe and secure place to puke their guts up. But as soon as I thought I was concealed, I let my feet carry me into a full-on sprint into the darkness.

Get away, I encouraged myself. *Get as far away as you can. Get back to Fortune Springs. Get back home.*

But his voice rose up behind me. Dammit. Caught.

"Where do you think you're going?"

I didn't respond. I was running too fast. Fighting against the forest and the shadows for my freedom.

"Hey! Hey!"

It was a minute later, when I thought I was in the clear, that I first smelled the smoke coming up the mountain behind me.

Now, I wasn't just outrunning the man. I was outrunning the flames from the lit cigarette he'd just tossed into the brush.

Chapter Twenty-Six

The mountain had never looked so ugly. Or so terrifying. But I pressed onward through the dark shapes, backlit by stars and haze. I pressed on as the smoke grew around me. As the footfall behind me grew louder and louder. As more and more pieces of the earth around me fell to the growing invasion of flames on either side. The weather had dried in the days since Owen and I had taken our lakeside refuge during a rainstorm and now the trees were going up like powder kegs.

The smoke was growing all around me, creating walls that forced me to move in ways I might have thought unconscionable a moment ago. But between the flames and the smoke and the man pursuing me from behind, I was just trying to find safe air now. Anything to be free again. Anything to live through this moment when every instinct in my body told me that I would be dead any minute now.

I didn't know how long I'd been running. I could only count the time by the intervals between the screams of the man tailing me.

"Virginia! V! Where are you? Come on. I know you don't want to get hurt any more than I want you to be hurt. Just come back down here and let's talk."

I'd started moving up the mountain now. Towards the rock faces above which I could see the only patch of star-dipped sky left. It wasn't much of an escape plan, but for now, I just wanted to live. And that seemed like my best bet. My only bet.

"V!"

As I ran, I tried not to think about this as my last moments. I didn't want to die scrambling in the dirt, gasping for clean air, as Porter chased me. I didn't want to die without saying a real goodbye to Calla and Willa and everyone else I'd met in Fortune Springs. Without holding my puppies one last time. But most of all, I didn't want to die without having told Owen I loved him.

Through the forest and the brush I pushed myself, dragging the neck of my T-shirt over my mouth to stop as much of the smoke from entering my lungs as I could. If I could just get some fresh air, if I could just get the smoke out of my lungs long enough to think straight again, to replace survival instincts with some clear thought—

Too late. It was too late to realize that I wasn't heading towards a clearing. I was heading towards a dead end. And I was cornered. A rock face ahead of me. Smoke behind me. Flames to the left of me. And a road to the right.

"There you are," he crowed, closing the gap between us. The light from the encroaching flames and the stars above us illuminated him. I stepped backwards, only to hit sold, immovable rock. Nowhere to run. "Did you really think I was just going to let you go?"

"Porter—"

A cold, dirty hand wrapped around my throat. A clenching snake determined to squeeze the breath out of me.

"Did you really think I would just let you humiliate me and get away with it? That I would waste all of the time, and effort, and *money* I threw at you?"

His eyes were wild. The fire reflected in them, and every second of his stare promised danger. Pain. The end of everything.

I tried to speak. "Please, stop—"

"You are so ungrateful, you know that? Is this what you wanted? Is this why you ran away? For the attention?"

Breathing was so hard now. Almost impossible. But if I was going to die right now—from the fire or the man—then I was going to go out fighting.

"No," I hissed. "I ran because I wanted to get the *hell* away from you."

Porter's eyes were full of tears. But from the emotion or the smoke, I couldn't tell. "I didn't want to hurt you."

But just as his hand tightened one last time, a voice—a voice I thought I would only be hearing in my dreams from now on—rose higher than the flames, filling the air more powerfully than the smoke.

"Well, don't worry. You aren't going to get the chance."

"*What?*"

Porter loosened his grip on me, but didn't release me completely. My heart filled with terror and hope, all at once. Terror that Owen was here, in the thick of danger, and hope that he was so close to me.

"Owen, no!"

But Owen didn't listen to my protest. Instead, he held out one hand in warning towards Porter, and kept all of his attention focused there. "Now, listen. My truck is down at the fire road. The rest of the fire department is working on the fires. You can come with me calmly, and we can turn you over to the proper authorities. Or, we can do this the hard way."

Porter barked a laugh; the smoke, which was quickly taking over all the fresh air in the area, made the sound sandpaper jagged. "And what way is that, water boy?"

"Since you ask, I can drag you through the flames and you can recover from your burns in a prison hospital bed."

"I don't think you're in any position to be negotiating here, friend. I've got the girl. And you've got nothing."

Owen's eyes flickered from Porter to mine. I swallowed hard. *Please don't do anything stupid*, I thought, *I love you too much to see you get hurt because of me.* But Owen merely smirked with a confidence that made my heart almost take flight.

"Is that what you think?"

"From where I'm standing, it looks pretty clear. Here's my counter-offer: you let me take Virginia, and we'll leave your quiet little backwater town in peace. How does that sound?"

Owen hadn't taken his eyes off of me. "Virginia?"

"Don't talk to her," Porter said, right as I coughed, "yes?"

"Stop, drop, and roll, okay?"

In any other situation, I would have furrowed my brow and questioned him. But for the briefest of confused seconds, Porter loosened his grip on me, and I knew I had to trust the man I loved with everything I had.

Gathering my energy, I did exactly as he instructed. I tensed my body, dropped to the forest floor, and let the momentum of my body do the rest, carrying me down the side of the rocky, painful hill until I came to an abrupt, slightly painful stop against a tree.

The smoke in my eyes and the pain in my lungs made everything after that difficult to see and process. It was like being half awake through a dream; I could see the pieces of reality before me, but they were all covered by a thick film, making comprehension almost impossible.

Porter screamed. From the fire road, a truck loosed a heavy bolt of water, knocking the man off of his feet. Visibly using all of his strength, Owen pinned the man to the ground, where he remained until a small team of similarly dressed firefighters came to retrieve the man from the ground, kicking and screaming and spluttering the whole way back to the truck in the distance.

The smoke grew, but the flames were getting smaller and smaller with each passing second. Just like me, whose heartbeat grew faster and faster despite the fact that my breaths became shallower and shallower.

I was going to die there, I realized. As I stared up through a small break in the smoke and trees above me to see a hole of clear, night sky, I knew that there was no path ahead for me. There was too much smoke in my lungs. The world seemed too distant, like I was already beginning the process of letting it go entirely.

I felt the pain. I felt the shortness of breath, the tension as my lungs struggled for more air I'd never be able to capture again. What I didn't feel was fear. Or sadness. Because I wasn't going to die alone. I wasn't going to die with Porter or by his hands. I was going to slip away in this beautiful forest, while the man I loved was holding my hand.

Vaguely I heard his voice calling out my name. Felt his other hand against my neck, searching for my weakening pulse. Eventually, I felt his lips press against mine as he tried to breathe life back into me, and I smiled.

The last thought I had as I let the darkness consume me? *Kissed by Owen Harris. What a way to go.*

Chapter Twenty-Seven

Vanilla. And smoke. Heaven—or hell, if that's where I'd ended up—smelled a lot like vanilla and smoke. As a matter of fact, through the faint scent of fire, wherever I had gone after slipping into darkness smelled remarkably like Calla's house on pancake day.

Heaven it was, then.

As I slowly regained consciousness, I didn't dare to open my eyes, but I slowly allowed more and more of the outside word to seep into my understanding. There was a heart monitor beeping somewhere nearby. The sound of someone's quiet breaths. The pain in my own chest. Something blocking the passages to my nose and helping me move air more evenly through my sore lungs.

I wasn't dead. At least, I was pretty sure I wasn't dead. And when I managed to barely open my eyes, I confirmed my suspicions.

Not dead. Not in a hospital, either. Just tucked into bed in my room in the Bride House. A breathing apparatus tucked into my nose, a monitor on my right index finger. And, at my bedside, a scowling man staring down at his hands.

Owen.

"You know," I said, struggling for the words with my raw, unused voice, "if you keep frowning like that, you'll get wrinkles."

Owen's head snapped up, and the relief, the joy on his face was enough to draw tears to my eyes almost instantly. "Virginia."

But he didn't say anything else. "I must really look bad if I've left you speechless. I don't think I've ever seen you at a loss for words before."

"You look very good for a woman who just went through hell."

"And you look pretty good for a man who saved me from it. Am I…" I scanned the room around me, not wanting to state the obvious but not wanting to be kept in the dark either. "I'm not in a hospital, am I?"

"Uh, no. Calla doesn't really trust hospitals. Or, rather, she doesn't really trust hospital billing departments. So, she called a few of her doctor friends from around the area and they all have been coming in and out to make sure you get the best care. I'm pretty sure even royalty doesn't get treatment this good."

"And the prognosis?"

"You're going to be fine. A little bit of bruising. Some soreness. The breathing machine was just to help you while you slept. You can take it out now, if you'd like. But other than that, you're expected to make a full recovery. They've even recommended a therapist for you to visit when you're physically feeling better."

"I'm supposed to be the therapist around here."

"Even therapists need therapy sometimes."

Yeah. I was sure of that now. It would do me good, I decided, to talk to someone about everything that had happened to me. To process all of the trauma and help break down the memories I would now have to live with for the rest of my life. Maybe the therapist would even let me bring one or two of the puppies along to the sessions, for comfort. After all, that's what I would do with my patients once I had them.

For the first time, I realized that going through therapy myself might make me better at my job. Go figure. I needed some help before I could help others. Strangely, the thought brought me comfort. It would be hard work, getting better. But I had survived so much. Fought through so much. Now, I was going to use that precious life I'd fought to protect and actually live it.

"Are we going to talk about it? About what happened?" I asked, after a long moment of silence.

Maybe it had been the wrong thing to ask, but I couldn't help it. My pictures of the entire event were fuzzy at best. I found myself grasping at fragments of memory and trying to piece them together… with barely any success. A shadow crossed Owen's face, deepening those frown lines I'd pointed out just a moment ago.

"I was in town when someone called to alert me about the smoke on the mountain. The man who attacked you confessed to flicking a lit cigarette into the forest, and we believe that's what started the blaze. When I called Calla to start the town phone tree, she told me you were on the mountain, and I sent most of the department to fight the blaze and took a small contingent with me to try and find you."

"And you did."

I would never forget that moment, when I blinked through the smoke and saw him standing there. Everything in me believed that I could have kept fighting to free myself from Porter if he hadn't shown up, but, boy, was I glad he had anyway.

"And we did," Owen said, nodding in agreement. He didn't meet my gaze, choosing instead to stare at a knot in the wood patterns on the floor. "We took one of the fire roads up the mountain, and when I saw him, I tried to get him to let you go peacefully. And when he wouldn't… I decided to hit him with one of our water canons. It knocked him out almost instantly. Made him pretty compliant after that."

"What happened to him?"

The worst parts of me wanted something awful to happen. For him to accidentally roll into a wall of flame and never be seen or heard from again. Or for a random lightning bolt to flash out of the sky and turn him into nothing more than an ash spot on the side of the road. The better parts of me—the parts I liked to believe were dominant—whispered that something so quick wouldn't be justice. He needed a long, healthy life to learn from his mistakes. To pay for how he'd hurt me.

"We turned him over to the county authorities. He won't be bothering you again."

I might have questioned that further had the vow come from anyone else's lips. But when Owen said it, I actually believed it. The fear rising up in my heart subsided. The monitor at my bedside slowed to a more manageable rate.

In the mostly-silence that followed, I watched as Owen kept his gaze tightly transfixed on our joined hands. He looked at them, sure, but he didn't really *see* them. It was more like he was staring through them, reliving memories instead of staying in this present with me. Dark circles colored half-moons beneath his eyes. His shoulders were slumped. I tried to put myself in his shoes.

"It must have been hard for you."

"What must have?"

I tightened my grip on his hands, reassuringly. "Attacking him like you did. I know how much your peace means to you. How much it means to you to *not* hurt anyone."

When he finally lifted his face to mine, there wasn't a trace of the guilt I expected to see in his expression. Instead, there was determination. A peace the likes of which I'd never seen in him before. He didn't regret his choice. In fact, I'd be willing to bet he would do it all over again, if given the chance.

"It does mean a lot to me. But you mean more."

Before I could realize what was happening, he'd brought my hand to his lips and pressed a kiss into the skin there. In that kiss, he gave me everything neither of us could say out loud. Neither of us dared. But we both felt it, and that was enough for now.

"Thank you."

"For what?"

"For saving me."

He chuckled, his smile unusually wide. I felt a smile of my own coming on, and I marveled at how the muscles in my face were now unused to the sensation. "I should be thanking you for the same thing."

"I didn't do anything but get myself in trouble."

"No, you've saved me in way more important ways than that. You've shown me that I don't have to be the person I was. That I really *can* grow. And change. And be better."

"You can. I think, now, maybe anyone can."

"Together?"

I nodded. "Together."

And with that, I didn't want to waste another second not kissing him. Using his hands to pull him even closer into me, I pressed my lips firmly against his, letting him breathe into me as we moved as one. That kiss was a reminder of life. The life I'd fought so hard to keep. And I savored every second of it.

But, too soon, a strange sound erupted at my closed bedroom door, and I pulled away. The combination of scratching and mewling wasn't letting up. "What is that?"

"Oh." The tips of Owen's ears went pink. "The puppies weren't doing so well without you. So, while I've been holding vigil here, they've been with me. We'd better let them in now that you're awake, hadn't we?"

I opened my mouth to answer, but another voice beat me to the punch. A voice from the other side of the door.

"Yes, you'd better."

"Calla?"

Without another word, the bedroom door swung open, and a deluge of human and puppy life flooded the space. Willa and Calla spilled into the room, as the Dalmatians made their way across the floor and struggled to hop onto the mountain of covers swaddling my body. The chaos was instant, but the warmth of the moment was, too, and I basked in all of it. Their conversations came in fragments like fireworks, hot and fast and too beautiful for words.

Calla: "I didn't think you were ever going to wake up. Not in the dead sense, but in the oversleeping sense, you know what I mean?"

Willa's eyes were wide and full of unshed tears. "I'm so glad you're okay."

"Darling, of course she was going to be okay. She's a Bride House girl. They're made of hardy stuff, you know."

The chaos continued all around us, with animals and friends and conversation that soon spiraled away from the tragedy of the last day and towards happier topics. Soon, the entire Bride House was nestled in my room, puppies in my lap and laughter on everyone's lips. It was then that I pulled Owen close one more time.

"Hey, Owen?"

"Yeah?"

"I love you."

"I love you, too."

For the first time in my life, I believed in those words. And I knew I would go on believing them for the rest of my life.

Epilogue

From the moment since I'd first arrived at the Bride House, I'd been looking forward to this day. When I'd first imagined it, my mind conjured up images of me strutting down the front steps in a noir-ish black dress and sunglasses, heading straight for a sporty roadster that would drive me directly out of this town and towards the sunshine and beaches of California. I'd always imagined that when this moment came, when the day finally arrived and my contract with the Bride House was over, when I left the place behind, that I would at last, feel free.

I imagined that leaving the house, suitcase and daydreams firmly in hand, would be liberating. That I would get in my car and never look back. That I would at the very least be *happy* about the prospect of never coming back to this place.

But as I stood in the front entryway, heat and a river of tears built up behind my eyelids. There was no way the woman I was a year ago would have known the woman I'd become now. The last year had changed me in ways that were impossible to predict. I'd gone from showing up here looking like the epitome of a teenage runaway—with my dark hoodie and backpack, shaking anytime someone so much as looked in my direction, desperate to get my money and get away to… well, this. A strong, confident woman with a lot of love in my heart. And almost no desire to leave the Bride House.

Unlike in my fantasies of this moment, I didn't strut straight out of the door or wear a long, black dress more appropriate for a funeral than a going away party. Instead, I shone in gold and white, a sundress I'd picked out just for this occasion. Lately, every time I'd so much as thought of leaving the Bride House, I felt a dark, gray cloud swirling over my head. The dress was my attempt to contradict that feeling and put me in a better place as I said goodbye.

I lingered in the front hallway. The backpack I'd brought here with me to the Bride House had been replaced by a suitcase and a handful of other knick-knacks and essentials I hadn't been able to fit in there, and the heft of it all weighed me down. From the dogs barking outside, I could tell that salvation—in the form of Owen and my van—was just a few steps away.

Still… I didn't want to say goodbye. Not just yet.

"What are you waiting for?"

By now, I should have been used to Calla sneaking up on me. But I'd been so lost in my own thoughts—trying to memorize the tuberose and coffee scent of the air here, trying to capture how the sun through the curtains danced across my skin—that I hadn't heard the woman creaking the floorboards as she approached. I turned to face her, blinking furiously to try and banish the tears quickly threatening to overtake me.

"Pardon?"

"I asked what you are waiting for. Did you forget something?"

From the look in Calla's eyes—all knowing, all seeing, all wisdom and humor in equal measures—she knew I hadn't forgotten a damn thing.

"No, I didn't forget anything."

That was all I could say without my voice breaking. I stopped the last word short to keep myself steady. From the far end of the parlor, Calla approached.

"Then what are you waiting for? There's nothing left for you here."

With that one statement, the sadness threatening to overtake me turned into something almost approaching rage. "Nothing left for me here? Calla, how could you even say that? This place... it's meant so much to me. You have to know that being here completely changed my life. I wouldn't be the person I am now without this old house, without Willa, without you—"

A roll of the eyes and a waving gesture of Calla's hand were enough to shut me up entirely. From anyone else, the gestures might have offended me, might have shored me up to fight even *harder* for my opinion. Not so with Calla. Somehow, that woman knew how to tell hard truths with soft, velvet lining. "I do know that. I know all of that. When you walked through that door for the first time, you were so beaten down, you didn't have anywhere to go but up."

"Yes, and—"

"And you've done so well for yourself." Her stern expression slipped into a small, affirming smile. "You've built your entire life back up from nothing. But you've gotten everything you could ever need from this place. I want you to keep growing, my dear, you've got to leave the pot and get out of the garden, you know?"

Of course. More gardening metaphors. At first, they'd slightly annoyed me, but now, I was suddenly gripped by the sadness that I would, from now on, probably go through most of my days without them. I took one of Calla's weathered, soft hands in my own. I decided to play along with the gardening metaphor. Just once. For old times' sake.

"But I like the flowerpot. And this gardener."

"Well." Calla hadn't ever been one for the mushy stuff. But she played along here, just for the moment, squeezing my hand right back. "This gardener loves you too much to let you stay. It's time to move on, my dear. I can't wait to see what beautiful, wonderful, world-shaking things you do with this life you've built for yourself."

All of that was true. I knew it in my heart. This house and the people in it—eccentric and strange as they were—had given me the opportunity to go out and make something of this one, precious life of mine. Staying here would be wasting that opportunity.

Knowing that it was true didn't make going through it any easier.

"But I'm going to miss you."

"Oh, please. I know you'll never be gone long. After all, you know where I hide the spare key."

True. But all the same, I couldn't miss the water now welling up in Calla's eyes. Emotions weren't her strong suit, but that didn't mean she didn't have them. In order to save her pride—and maybe because I really, really wanted to and didn't think I'd ever get another opportunity—I threw my arms around the older woman and pulled her in for a tight hug. Saving us both the embarrassment of crying in front of each other.

"Goodbye, Calla. Thank you so much. For everything. I can't ever—"

"You can thank me by going out and doing the damn thing. I didn't help you just so you could stay here forever. Letting go is hard. But it's the reason we fight so hard in the first place."

"You're right."

I could practically hear the smile in the older woman's voice. "I usually am."

"I just—I—It's just that I really—"

The tears threatened again. My voice didn't hold up to the emotions they were trying to support. Wet, salty teardrops fell down my cheeks.

"I know." Calla held me tighter, wrapping in that hug all of her unspoken hopes and dreams and wishes for my future. I felt them all in that embrace and tried to soak them in, to hold on to them forever. "I really love you too."

Neither of us said goodbye. After all, it wasn't goodbye, was it? I would be moving a few miles down the road, and Calla would still be here in the Bride House, hopefully opening the doors to a new crop of young women soon. We'd see each other soon. We'd still be close.

This wasn't goodbye. It was just *I'll see you later*. And that knowledge helped me lift my chin, collect my things, and finally make my way out of the door.

Sure enough, outside, the sun practically gushed down onto the small town. Fortune Springs completely reflected its name—a place where hope and future and good luck poured forth like water from a thawed-out creek. I glanced over at the porch swing, where Willa and one of her new friends from school were busy poring over a stack of textbooks for their upcoming exams. I offered Willa a wave and a smile. She returned them both, before promptly sticking her tongue out at me.

With a laugh, I moved my gaze from her and back out across the lawn. Owen had parked my van in front of the dark wrought-iron gates, and leaned against it so he could look up at me as I descended the steps. When our eyes met, his smile broadened—giving my heart one of its trademark Owen Harris flutters—and the small cavalcade of puppies in the front seat of the van whipped into a delighted frenzy.

All of the worry and sadness of leaving the Bride House withered away, leaving only warmth and light in their place. I wasn't leaving anything behind. I wasn't running away from anything anymore. Instead, I was walking—confidently, happily, excitedly—towards something. Towards my future. Towards my happiness. Towards Owen.

After greeting all the pups individually and slipping my things into the back of the van, I pulled myself into the front seat beside Owen, where I kissed him like I'd never kissed him before.

When my lips were tingling and I needed to come up for air, he cradled my cheek and searched my eyes.

"How are you holding up?"

It took me a moment of consideration before I could respond. Not because I didn't know how to answer his question, but because now, there were happy tears pooling in my eyes. The kind of tears that only came when you couldn't control or bottle up your own joy. "You know what? I think I'm better than ever."

And I looked forward to things getting better and better... for the rest of my life.

A Letter from Alys Murray

Dear reader,

I want to say a huge thank you for choosing to read *Small Town Secrets*. If you did enjoy it, and want to keep up to date with all my latest releases, just sign up at the following link. Your email address will never be shared and you can unsubscribe at any time.

www.bookouture.com/alys-murray

I truly hope you enjoyed your time in Fortune Springs, Colorado as much as I did. Writing about the Bride House brought me so much happiness during the trash fire year of 2020, and I hope it gave you a little bit of warmth, joy, and escape in 2021.

If Virginia's story resonated with you, I encourage you to donate to a domestic violence hotline, shelter, or support foundation in your local area. During this unprecedented time, people in toxic relationships have fewer resources than ever to escape their situations; your generosity could help save someone's life.

Finally, I hope you loved *Small Town Secrets* and if you did, I would be very grateful if you could write a review. I'd love to hear what you think, and it makes such a difference helping new readers to discover one of my books for the first time.

I love hearing from my readers—you can get in touch on my Facebook page, through Twitter, Goodreads or my website.

Thanks,
Alys

                               alysmurrayauthor

                               @writeralys

                               @writeralys

                               18155460.Alys_Murray

Acknowledgments

2020 was the wrong year to write a book. I got stuck in a foreign country (Portugal) during the first wave of lockdowns, had to escape to Greece when my allowed time in Portugal expired, and mostly wrote this book while wedged, on the floor, in a small spot of lamplight between the bed and the wall of my Airbnb.

But, somehow, in the midst of this year's madness, I managed to write a few books. Every book is a miracle, of course, but in 2020 it feels even more so. And this miracle wouldn't have been possible without Emily Gowers, the world's best editor and a true friend. We started our publishing together in 2019, and I would not be the author I am without her guidance, her encouragement, her friendship, and her willingness to fangirl about the cancelled television series *Timeless*.

Other miracle workers on this current book include my mother (who endured countless Facebook Messenger meltdowns while I was quarantined in Europe), the rest of my family (who endured the same, but over FaceTime), Stacey, Jana, Sophie, and everyone who wrote the books, television, movies, and musicals that got me through this incredibly difficult and strange time. And, as always, this book wouldn't exist without Adam, my husband. This life is an adventure, and there's no one I'd rather be on this adventure with than you.

Made in the USA
Coppell, TX
29 March 2021

52592304R00148